DANCING WITH THE DOC

JENNIFER YOUNGBLOOD

CRAIG DEPEW, MD

ARBOR
HOUSE

YOUR FREE BOOK AWAITS

Get Beastly Charm: A Contemporary retelling of beauty & the beast as a welcome gift when you sign up for my newsletter. You'll get information on my new releases, book recommendations, discounts, and other freebies.

Get the book at:

http://bit.ly/freebookjenniferyoungblood

PROLOGUE

Carmelita skipped joyfully down the sidewalk, her new blue gingham dress swishing in the breeze as she sang on the way to the bus stop. She kicked the leaves that had fallen overnight from the white oak trees between the street and the sidewalk. With an exaggerated wave of her hand above her head, she spun in circles, the skirt of her dress spreading out in a blur around her. Her pigtails swung back and forth, slapping her shoulders. Carmelita loved to dance. If she could forget about school and all the stupid homework and just spend the rest of her life dancing, she'd be happy.

"Hi, Cat," someone called out. She turned and saw her best friend running down the front steps of her house, carrying a notebook and pink Barbie lunch box.

"Miss Miriam, I presume," Carmelita said with a mock curtsy. "Carmelita Andrea Anastasia Hernandez de Silva at your service."

"I prefer Cat," Miriam replied, breathless from running down her front walk. She looked Carmelita up and down. "Nice dress."

"Thank you," she responded with a burst of pride. "My mami got paid yesterday. We bought it last night. Like it, huh?"

"Yup. You look great."

Carmelita turned up her chin and walked regally ahead of Miriam. "I know," she crooned. "You may now proceed to admire me."

Miriam giggled. Half a block ahead, a commotion was erupting at the bus stop. Two boys were holding another, his arms pinned behind his back. Their prisoner was yelling at the top of his lungs. "Stop it! Let go of me! That's not your pack. Give it back!"

A third bully, even larger than the other two, zipped open the trapped boy's backpack. He reached in and pulled out a fist full of papers, which he threw backwards over his head into the street. A car drove by, scattering them. He reached in again and pulled out an envelope.

The girls had gotten close enough to hear the bully's taunts. Carmelita recognized the bully—Drew O'Hannon. Two grades ahead of Carmelita, Drew was as mean as he was tough. "Aww, wookie. Mommy puts your wunch money in a wittle envelope so it won't get lost. How sweet." He chortled out a heartless laugh. One of his henchmen let go of the victim with his left hand and gave Drew a high five. Drew tore open the envelope and poured the coins into his hand.

"Nice, Chase. Thanks." He slid the lunch money into his right front pocket. Then, he yanked Chase's arm back, and swung a fist into Chase's stomach. "But it's not enough. Tomorrow bring more. My boys here will have to go hungry today, but I know that tomorrow you'll have something for them too, won't you?"

Rage filled Cat. Not only was Chase her friend, but she'd secretly had a crush on him since the start of the school year. "Let him go," she demanded.

The chumps holding Chase's arms let go. Chase fell to the ground, clutching his stomach. He looked up at the bully, eyes blazing. "You're a scab, O'Hannon!"

"What did you say?" Drew kicked Chase's side before rolling him over on his back. In a flash, he jumped onto Chase's chest. His arm went back to deliver a blow to the face, but the fist never connected. A blue blur streaked across the space as Carmelita leapt on Drew, knocking him off Chase.

Carmelita scratched and clawed for all she was worth, but she was no match for the much larger sixth grader. In a flash, Carmelita was on her back, Drew on top, pressing her arms against the ground. "If you wasn't a girl, I'd …" He paused as if unsure how to finish.

Cat struggled but couldn't get free. She glared up. "Let me go, Drew O'Hannon. I'll poke your eyes out."

Drew laughed. "You stupid little PR. You can't do anything to me."

"I'm not Puerto Rican. And you're gravely mistaken if you think I won't do anything to you."

There was a squeal of brakes, signaling that the bus had arrived. The doors hissed open as the driver observed the scene. Immediately, he picked up a radio microphone. "Police dispatch, we have a youth situation at the bus stop, one-oh-nine-one-two south Devonshire. Need a couple of units here immediately." He hung the mike in its cradle and remained in his seat, not willing to leave the bus to help.

Drew placed a big paw over Cat's face. He ground the back of her head into the grass and laughed some more. She squirmed to get away but stopped when she felt the cloth of her new dress ripping underneath her.

Through a gap between Drew's meaty fingers Cat could see curious students watching out of the bus windows, but no one got off to help. Drew leaned up on his toes so he could put more weight on her face.

Cat knew where to kick a boy to get his attention. She had her pointy-toed black church shoes on with her dress, and when the police arrived a few seconds later Drew was rolling on the ground, holding his crotch. His lackeys might have released Chase and grabbed Cat had the authorities not arrived when they did.

"You guys got here fast," the bus driver commented.

"We were just up the street on our break. These kids are making us miss breakfast," an officer with stripes on his sleeve complained. "Okay, what happened?" Three other officers moved into position, surrounding the kids.

The bus driver spoke. "Those two grabbed that one. The big one stole the kid's lunch money and started beating him up. Then the little girl attacked the ring leader. You shoulda seen it."

A female officer look admiringly at Cat. "You did that?"

Cat just nodded.

An officer stepped up to Drew and held out his hand. "Fork it over." Drew dug into his pocket and pulled out the contents. "I'll take that," the officer said as he scooped the pocket knife out of Drew's hand. He pointed to Chase. "Give him back the money." Drew said nothing. He just passed the lunch money to Chase.

The officer turned back to the driver. "You say these two are okay?" he asked, looking at Cat and Chase

The bus driver's eyes widened. "They're more than okay. If I was getting mugged, I'd want her on my side."

The officer jerked his thumb toward the bus. "Okay, you guys get on the bus and get out of here. Don't be late for school." He grabbed Drew by the back of his collar and glared at the others. "You three, into my car, now. We're going to go find your mothers."

Cat smiled when she saw one of Drew's lackeys go instantly pale. It was obvious that he was far more scared of his mama than the police. Once she and Chase were on the bus, the doors hissed closed and the driver pulled onto the road. Chase caught her eye. His expression of gratitude almost made getting her dress ripped worth it.

A few weeks later, on a fairly nondescript Tuesday, Cat had just left her house to go to the bus stop. She was on the edge of her yard when a scrap of white paper caught her eye. It was wedged into the knothole of a tree. Curiously, she went over and pulled it out. The paper was folded into a neat square. She glanced around. There was no one else in sight. She opened it, her breath catching when she read the first words.

Dear Cat,

What? It was a letter to her? She read it again.

Dear Cat,

I love the way you dance. You're so fun to watch. I could never have moves like that. You should go pro someday. Hero.

That was all it said. She looked around again. As far as she could tell, no one was watching from the houses. Standing on her tiptoes, she peered into the knothole, surprised that there were more scraps of paper. She pulled out the next one. It was hard and slightly yellowed.

Dear Cat,

I'm sorry you were sick with the flu. I hope you feel better. Hero.

She frowned. It had been almost three weeks since she'd had the flu. The note had been through several days of rain and wind during that time.

She reached into the hole again and grabbed a handful of notes. One looked really old.

Dear Cat,

I think you're cool. Hero.

She crinkled her nose. She didn't know anyone named *Hero*. Was he referring to himself as some kind of superhero? She flipped through the notes, some more faded with age than others.

Dear Cat,

My mom made me eat beets last night. They were gross.

Okay. No real information in that one.

There were eighteen in all. One was a faded Valentine card.

Dear Cat,

I sent Valentines to my whole class but the person I really wanted to send one to is you. Hero.

How sweet. Someone had a crush on her but was too shy to say anything in person. She had to know who it was. How could she find out? Stuffing the notes into her pocket, she hurried to the stop to catch the bus. She got there before the last kids climbed on. Cat went down the aisle to sit next to Miriam. "Look what I found," Cat said in a low tone as she pulled the notes from her pocket.

"Where did you find them?"

"They were wedged into the hole in the tree in front of my house."

Miriam's eyes sparkled with adventure as she took the paper on top of the stack and began reading, "'Dear Cat,' Nice opening," she said with a giggle. "'I like your new hair style.'" Miriam made a face. "When did you get a new hair style?"

Cat tried to think. "Last time I got a haircut was in the summer, more than three months ago. That's the thing. These notes look like they've been coming for a really long time ... like years."

"Who's Hero?"

She shrugged. "Your guess is as good as mine."

"Cat's got a boyfriend! Cat's got a boyfriend," Miriam sang out.

"Shh! I don't have a boyfriend," she hissed. "Besides, he can't be my boyfriend if I don't even know who he is."

"Let me see another one." Miriam snatched the next note from Cat's hand and started reading. "'Dear Cat, How's it going? Hero.' Look at the nice heart he drew. How romantic." Her voice had a teasing tone.

Cat turned the pile over and picked up what had to be the oldest note from the bottom of the stack. The paper was so brittle and weathered that a corner broke off when she unfolded it. "Wow. Red crayon. How old is this?" The handwriting looked like it belonged to a kindergartener. "'Dear Carmalitta.'" She sighed. "How come nobody around here knows how to spell my name?" Now, most people knew her as Cat, but when she was younger everyone called her Carmelita. She continued reading. "'You're nice and priddy. Can we be frinds?'" There were two boxes ... a yes and no. It was signed Hero. She pursed her lips. "Even back then he was calling himself Hero."

"I guess *Superman* was already taken," Miriam teased.

The bus slowed down and pulled to the side of the street in front of the school. Cat got off the bus, still pondering over the notes. Who was Hero? She looked at the masses of students congregating beneath the breezeway, waiting for school to begin. Was Hero here?

Cat went to place the notes back into her pocket, but the wind caught one and sent it sailing across the yard in front of the school.

"Oh no," Miriam moaned. "We'll never catch it."

The note skimmed the ground to the far side of the schoolyard and would have escaped through the fence had a boy not stomped his boot down, trapping it. They watched as he bent over and picked it up. When they could see his face, they gasped. It was Drew. He was the last person they wanted in on their secret.

"We'll never get it back from him," Miriam groaned.

Despair sank over Cat. Which one of the notes did Drew have? One with her name on it? How many Cats were there in the school? She had no idea. Not wanting Drew to see her nearby and connect the note to her, she grasped Miriam's arm. "Don't worry about it. Let's go inside."

The notes kept coming all that school year and into the next. Sometimes they were flirty, sometimes sad, always anonymous. Cat was dying to know who Hero was, but it seemed that the person was being very careful to never give any clues about his identity. They didn't come every day, but at least a handful each month, and often, a few times a week there was a surprise waiting for her in the tree.

Winter came and went. Spring arrived in an explosion of color. Chicago's famous winds ripped blossoms from the trees and sent them cascading in waves down the street. They gave Cat all the more reason to dance as she leapt over and through the tumbling masses of petals rolling in the wind.

As Cat left for school, she stopped by the tree. There hadn't been anything there for over a week. When she spotted the slip of paper, a smile curved her lips as she hungrily read it.

Dear Cat,

Sorry about all the notes. I promise I'm not a stalker. I just like having someone to talk to. If you hate the notes and want me to stop, just put a rock in the knothole, and I won't send any more. But I hope you don't. Hero.

Stop? Why would she want him to stop? The notes were great. They made her feel special. She'd been checking the tree every morning hoping for more. She wouldn't have minded if Hero sent one every day. This past week, she'd begun to fear that Hero had lost interest in her. Tucking the note in her pocket, Cat went to the bus stop. When she returned home that afternoon, she got out a piece of paper and pen and started writing.

Dear Hero. Who are you? I have to know. I'm in Mrs. Nelson's class. Are you in her class too? I love your notes.

Wait! She'd used the word *love*. That wouldn't do. She crumpled up the paper and got another one.

Dear Hero. Thanks for the notes you've sent me. They mean a lot. It's been really hard for Mami and me without Dad here. Do you have two parents? I mean, do both of them live with you? I hope your life is happy, and I want to meet you. From Cat.

She folded the paper in half, and folded that in half again. With a nimble step, she hurried out to the tree to place it in the knothole. She smiled thinking of Hero's reaction when he realized that she'd written back. On more than one occasion, she'd looked out the window at the tree, hoping to catch a glimpse of Hero, but he was too stealthy.

She hardly slept a wink that night, wondering how Hero would answer. To her disappointment, there was no note. When Cat and Miriam got off the bus at school, the breezeway was empty because it was raining. They ran to the school entrance with all the rest of the kids while teachers clutching umbrellas urged them inside. Cat went to her locker to retrieve her books. As she closed the door, she was surprised to see Drew O'Hannon there.

"Hi, Cat."

It was hard to tell if he was sneering or smiling. She shrank back.

"I see you found my notes."

Her mouth went dry. Somehow, she managed to find her voice. "What notes?"

"The ones in the tree," he said smugly.

Her heart began to pound. No, this couldn't be happening! Hero couldn't be Drew O'Hannon. Drew was a blockheaded bully. He couldn't possibly be so sensitive and insightful. Had he been toying with her the entire time, or was Drew different inside than his outer shell?

He leaned closer. "Do you like them?"

Confusion swirled in Cat's head.

"It was kind of you to write back." Drew held up a sheet of paper —her note that she'd placed in the knothole this morning.

Her heart clutched as she tried to reconcile Hero with Drew O'Hannon. It was impossible. Her mind simply couldn't do it.

She clutched her book to her chest. "I—I've got to get to class."

"Be sure and drop me a note anytime," Drew said glibly with a wink. "You know our secret spot."

A wave of nausea rolled over Cat as she turned and hurried away, eager to put as much space between her and Drew O'Hannon as possible. There was no way she would ever leave a note for Drew O'Hannon. Her heart cracked.

Hero was dead.

1

Cat paced back and forth across the kitchen floor. "Are you sure you heard correctly?" She stopped and looked at the silver-haired woman sitting at the table, watching her with sympathetic eyes.

Romina nodded, a solemn expression on her lined face. "Juanita Garza saw Drew at the diner with another woman." She motioned with her hands. "The woman had big blonde hair and a tight red dress that left little to the imagination." Her face colored as she shook her head slowly back and forth. "I knew that Drew O'Hannon was trouble. You should've never gotten involved with him. If your mother saw you now, she'd roll over in her grave." She made a cross over her chest.

Romina had told Cat about the other woman a couple of hours ago, but Cat had been too upset to get the details, which was why she was asking Romina to repeat the story. Cat ran a hand through her hair, swallowing down the lump in her throat. "I can't believe Drew would do this to me." Actually, it wasn't so hard to believe. Ever since Cat had started dating Drew in her sophomore year in high school, she'd caught whispers of Drew's infidelity off and on. She'd confronted Drew about it, but he adamantly denied it. Midway through her junior year, Cat and Drew started fighting a lot. Drew was growing increasingly possessive and began cutting Cat down, chipping away at her confidence. Cat had planned to break up with Drew, but then her mom suddenly got sick with breast cancer and died. The house where Cat and her mother lived was a rental. There was no life insurance, no nest egg. Cat was a high school student without a penny to her name. She'd hadn't seen hide nor hair of her dad since he was deported. She'd been eight years old at the time.

With no money, Cat was afraid she'd have to give up dance, but her instructor Mrs. Patterson insisted that she keep coming to class. Cat paid her tuition by teaching junior classes. A few days after her mother's funeral, Cat moved in with her next-door neighbor Romina Castaneda, a widow who'd been her mom's best friend. It was just easier at that point to let things with Drew ride. Also, Cat had felt so alone that she needed someone to cling to. Drew played the part of the doting boyfriend so well that Cat assumed they'd moved past the rocky phase of their relationship and were on their way to building something lasting. Then, the rumors started up again.

"Sit down," Romina encouraged. "You're making me nervous with all that pacing."

Huffing out a breath, she pulled out a chair and slumped down. Cat let out a harsh laugh. "You know what? I'm not shattered by Drew's infidelity." She gritted her teeth. "I'm mad enough to chew nails, but I'm not shattered." She sucked in a quick breath. "I guess I'm just mad at myself for letting it go on for so long." Maybe a part of her had wanted to believe that Drew really was the hero he pretended to be in his notes. The knothole, those notes ... they'd meant something to Cat. She'd even kept them. Remembering the notes made her think of a softer, kinder Drew. "I guess it's time I grew up and realized that Hero really is dead," she sighed.

Romina looked puzzled. "I'm sorry?"

She offered a wistful smile. "Never mind." Tears rose in her eyes as she fidgeted with her hands. "What am I gonna do?" She'd graduated from high school three months prior. Mrs. Patterson had asked her if she wanted to come on as a full-time dance instructor at the studio. While that was tempting, Cat was starting to feel like this neighborhood was suffocating her. Every time she looked at her former house, a deep sadness filled her. She thought of Mami ... how quickly the cancer took her life. Mami's life had been hard and sad. She'd worked three jobs to keep a roof over her and Cat's heads. Was it wrong to want something more? In a strange way, Drew's notes in the knothole had kindled a fire in Cat. They'd opened a space inside her that allowed her to dream of a new life with the possibility of a bright future with a hero who loved her for who she was. Not one who constantly tried to make her into something else. Her brow furrowed as she thought of Drew. All he cared about was being a jock. He craved the admiration of prominent people. Nothing Cat ever did was good enough for him. If she wore her hair a certain way, he wanted it another. If she wore a particular dress, he found something wrong with it.

Romina gave her a perceptive look. "You already know what you need to do. You're just trying to muster up the courage to do it."

Cat's head snapped up. "What do you mean?"

"You need to get away from here ... away from Drew. You need to find your own life."

Tears welled in her eyes. "It's true," she croaked. "It's just ..." Her words lost air as she tried again. She balled her fist, her fingernails digging into her palm. "I'm scared." There it was. She'd admitted it out loud.

Romina nodded. "I know." A tender smile spread over her thin lips. "But your mother will be watching over you from above. Never forget that."

Tears dribbled down Cat's cheeks as she nodded. She thought of something else. "How can I leave you?"

Romina patted her hand. "Don't worry about me. I'll be fine. I've got my kids close by."

A feeling of excitement trickled over Cat. Where would she go? Someplace warm. Florida. Mami had always talked of going to Florida but never got the chance. A new thought took hold, bringing back the gloom. "I don't have enough money." She'd squirreled away some, but it wasn't near enough to move.

Romina used her hands to heave herself to her feet. She shuffled over and opened a door to the cupboard. Pushing her flour and corn-meal canisters aside, she retrieved a jelly jar. Her arthritic fingers worked to unscrew the lid. She reached in and pulled out a wad of cash. A large, gleeful smile filled her face as she turned to Cat. "How much do you need?"

"Thank you," Cat breathed, tears running rivers down her cheeks. Her heart was filled to overflowing for this stooped, unassuming woman. "I'll leave in the morning," she sniffed, mopping her eyes. A second later, Cat about jumped out of her skin at the loud pounding on the door. She looked at Romina, whose face was carved with worry. "It's probably Drew," Cat said unnecessarily. They both knew it was him.

Less than an hour prior, Cat had called Drew and told him it was over. He'd yelled, screamed, and called her every name in the book until finally, she hung up on him.

"Don't answer the door," Romina warned, clutching the jar tightly in her hands.

More banging.

A white-hot anger rose in Cat's breast. "I'll not be bullied by Drew," she seethed. "Don't worry," she assured Romina, "it's really over this time." Running a hand through her hair and adjusting her clothes, she went to the door, trying to slow her erratic pulse.

"Open up, Cat," Drew demanded, pounding on the door with his fist. "We need to talk."

She flung it open, causing him to fall in. He caught himself and closed the door behind him. Then he got a good look at her tear-stained face. He swore under his breath. "I don't know what you've heard, but it's a lie. Baby," he began, touching her cheek.

She pushed his hand away. "Don't."

"Will you just listen to me?" he demanded.

Cat thought of Romina in the kitchen. Romina was frightened by Drew and his outbursts. "Let's go outside and talk on the front steps."

Before he could protest, she opened the door and went outside, leaving him no alternative but to follow. It was a dark night with only hints of the fingernail of a moon showing through the fast-moving clouds. Cat sat down on the steps, pulling her knees to her chest as she hugged them with her arms. Drew plopped beside her. She could feel him watching her. He trailed his fingers over the naked skin of her arm. "Cat," he began in a sultry tone that was probably supposed to be sexy, but it came across as grating.

She jerked her arm away. "Don't you dare touch me!"

Drew scowled. "You're being ridiculous. I told you there was no one else."

"People saw you in the diner," she snapped, the anger returning full force. "You were with a big-haired blonde with a skimpy red dress."

He blinked a few times in surprise, and she could see the guilt written all over his face. It made her sick to her stomach. She couldn't believe she'd wasted so much time on Drew.

His words rushed out in a heap. "It's not what you think. Monica works at the dealership. We were getting lunch for everyone."

A hard amusement tickled Cat's insides. Drew's dad owned a string of car dealerships. Drew's wealth had made him a big man on campus, making Drew think he could buy anything he wanted ... including her. Well, those days were over. Cat had thought him so handsome with his muscular build and thick crop of wavy, blonde hair. His quick smile and hazel eyes had turned many a head in high school. Drew was a bully when they were kids. If it hadn't been for his notes, Cat never would've given him the time of day. However, she'd started to view Drew differently. And even though no further notes were exchanged between them in the knothole, she took note of him. Then, when Drew asked her out, she accepted and the two fast became the *it couple* in school. Now, however, Cat was becoming disenchanted with Drew's looks. She wanted more than a good-looking face and monster-sized ego. She wanted a partner in life— someone to build her up and share her dreams. Drew was not that person. He cared nothing for her dance or the movies and books she enjoyed. Furthermore, Cat didn't fit in with Drew's country club life and fast friends.

"Drew, I'm tired of your lies. I'm not an idiot. I know there have been others. It's over."

His eyes narrowed. "Don't say that."

The fight had drained out of her. Drew's infidelity didn't matter. She was moving on. She ran her hands through her hair, feeling weary to the bone. "It's late, Drew. I need to get some rest."

"No," he countered, his jaw hard. "You're not going to bed until we work this out."

She grunted. "Get it through your thick skull. We're through." She stood. He sprang to his feet and caught her arm, his fingers digging into her flesh. "Let go of me," she growled.

He smirked. "Or what?"

"You're hurting me, Drew." She glanced around, wishing there were other people outside. It was just the two of them, however.

A mask of anger twisted Drew's face, and then she saw something that struck fear into the center of her heart—a smug look that let her know that Drew liked that she was afraid of him. It gave him some sick feeling of power. "I trusted you," she heaved through gritted teeth, tears rising in her eyes. "You took that trust and stomped it into the ground."

"Don't you talk to me like that, you little tramp." His breath seethed through his teeth as he spit out the angry words.

She winced at the stench of beer on his breath. "You're drunk," she said, disgust twisting her gut. His words stung, and she wasn't going to take it ... not anymore. "Go home, Drew." She grunted. "I never should've let you into my life. You're a low-down, cheating jerk!" Her voice escalated. "We're done!"

The hard slap took her by surprise. Pain wrenched through her as her head snapped back. The breath left her lungs, her mind reeling to process what had just happened. Drew had hit her! She wasn't one of those women. This couldn't be happening! Tears burned her eyes. "I hate you!"

He punched her in the jaw. She toppled backwards, holding her jaw. "Just leave," she cried.

Grabbing her hair, he yanked her to her feet and began dragging her down the steps.

"Stop!" she screamed, hitting his hand, but it was useless. "Where are you taking me?"

"You belong to me, and it's about time you acted like it."

Panic engulfed her, her legs wobbling uncontrollably. Drew had been pushing her to be intimate with him, but she'd put him off. It was with a sickening dread that she realized he intended to rape her.

"Stop right there!" Romina's thin, raspy voice filled the night air, bringing Cat a swift relief that left her dizzy.

"Go back inside, old woman," Drew roared.

Romina stood in a battle stance, holding up the phone. "I called the police."

Cat sensed Drew's hesitation and felt the tide shift. He released her, giving her a look filled with such hatred that it shriveled her insides. "This is not over," he sneered as he stormed down the walkway, got in his Mustang, and squealed off. Cat's legs were so weak she feared they might give way. She stumbled towards Romina, a sob trembling from her lips. Frail, meek Romina was her angel.

"Are the police coming?" Cat stammered as they rushed inside and locked the door. She dreaded having to talk to the police but knew it was inevitable.

Romina winced. "About that ... I might've fudged the truth a little."

Cat's eyes rounded as she hiccuped a laugh. "You were bluffing?" Her hand went to her mouth. She realized she was shaking all over.

Romina nodded. Her features pulled into taut lines, eyes darting towards the door, as if she feared Drew might break through it at any moment. "You need to leave ... tonight."

"Tonight?" Terror streaked through Cat. Her jaw throbbed with pain. Gingerly, she touched it, thinking she needed to put an ice pack on it.

Romina looked her in the eye. "You need to get as far away from this place and Drew O'Hannon as you can. Go someplace where he'll never find you." She placed a hand on Cat's arm, eyes cutting into hers. "Promise me."

"I promise," she croaked.

The future was a dark pool of muddy water. Facing it alone terrified Cat. Yet, staying here at Drew's mercy was even worse. She straightened her shoulders, trying to calm her pounding heart. Before she even consciously realized what she was doing, her silent plea lifted to heaven. *Help me*, she prayed. *Please, help me find my way.*

2

Cat was glad it was nighttime when she left. She didn't think her heart could take seeing the Chicago skyline vanishing in her rearview mirror as she headed south down the Interstate. When she'd moved out of her childhood home, Cat donated or threw away most of the mismatched furniture. She'd held onto a few keepsakes such as photo albums and a couple of Mami's dresses, mainly because they smelled like Mami, an earthy muskiness. All of this fit in a single box that Cat placed in the car, along with her things. Kind of sad, but Cat's entire life's belongings could easily fit in the trunk and backseat of the car with room to spare. When she crossed the state line out of Illinois, she blew a kiss. "Thanks for the good times," she said wistfully, blinking to stay the moisture in her eyes.

It was a little after ten p.m. when Cat left Romina's house and started out on her trip. Not wanting to waste her precious funds on a hotel, Cat intended to drive the entire way. However, around three a.m. her eyelids grew heavy, and she kept dozing off. With a jerk, she'd wake herself up, relieved that she'd not veered off the road. She rolled down the windows, turned up the music on the radio, and even kept her right foot raised an inch over the accelerator. Nothing helped. Finally, around four a.m., she pulled into a rest area. After making a quick trip to the restroom, she reclined her seat and drifted off into a heavy slumber wrought by emotional and physical exhaustion.

When she awoke, ribbons of pink were threaded through the morning sky. She went to the restroom again. This time, she brushed her teeth and attempted to smooth down her tangled curls before getting back on the road. Romina had packed her a few snacks. She munched on granola bars and an apple. Six hours later, her stomach impatiently asked for something else to eat. She'd eaten most of the snacks and didn't think she could stomach another granola bar. She spotted a green exit sign on the right shoulder of the road. "Clementine, one mile," she read aloud. "Sounds like a decent place to grab a bite." She got off at the exit.

As she pulled into the downtown district, she marveled at the neat rows of homes with large wraparound porches. It looked like something out of a picture. She'd almost stopped at the Dixie Freeze on her way in but wanted something healthier, so she ventured into the heart of town. As she drove around a quaint square, she saw a sign for a restaurant that read *The Magnolia*. Cat had been hoping for a sandwich shop. This might be too expensive. She'd better keep driving. A second later, steam started pouring from beneath her hood. Panic gripped her as she pulled into an empty parking space and cut off the engine. Her stomach twisted into a hard knot, tears pressing against her eyes. She got out and opened the hood, jumping back as a steam cloud mushroomed. It smelled like burned honey. *Don't panic*, she ordered herself. *One step at a time!*

"I'm not a mechanic, but I know that smell. Radiator fluid. You've either blown your radiator or busted a hose. Either way, you can't drive that thing anywhere until it gets fixed."

Cat straightened, looking to her side as a blonde woman in her mid to late twenties stepped up beside her. Her hunter green button-down shirt was embroidered with *The Magnolia* above a white flower. She extended her hand. "Harper Wallentine."

Swallowing the dryness in her throat, Cat took the offered hand. "Cat. Nice to meet you." Cat's voice sounded as shaky and unsettled as she felt. If this woman—Harper—was correct in her assessment of the car, then Cat was stuck here. She'd have to hire a mechanic to fix her car, which would eat into money that was supposed to be used to put a deposit down on an apartment. Fear nipped at her as she clutched her hands. She realized with a start that Harper was speaking.

"Cat? Like the furry thing that chases mice?"

It took Cat's tired brain a second to make the connection. They'd been talking about her name. "Carmelita Andrea Anastasia Hernandez de Silva. My friends call me Cat," she said automatically, unable to squelch the tears.

Harper chuckled. "I can see why." Concern touched Harper's features. "Honey, are you okay?"

Cat bit her lower lip as a hot embarrassment cloaked her. She was falling apart in front of a stranger ... in the center of town. She shook her head, tears slipping from her eyes. "I didn't count on this expense," she sniffed.

"No one ever does," Harper said sagely, giving her a measured look. "Why don't you come on inside the restaurant? You can eat something while you let your car cool down. Meanwhile, I'll see if I can scrounge up a mechanic."

"I don't want to be any trouble."

Harper flashed a warm smile. "No trouble at all." She glanced at the car's front license plate. "Illinois, huh? I thought I detected a slight Northern accent."

Cat didn't doubt that because in her ears, Harper had an exaggerated Southern twang like people in the movies. She pronounced Illinois with an S on the end, whereas Cat called it *Illanoy*.

Curiosity lit Harper's eyes. "Whereabouts are you from in Illinois?"

"Chicago," she answered and could tell Harper wanted more. "I left last night, heading for Florida."

Harper nodded. "We get a lot of business from tourists passing through." She opened the door and waved Cat inside the quaint restaurant. "Have a seat. Are you hungry?"

Cat's stomach rumbled at the question.

Hearing it, Harper laughed. "I'll be right back. In the meantime, sit down and make yourself at home."

"Thank you," Cat said, immensely grateful for Harper's kindness. Her mami had been a religious woman and took Cat to church every week. When Mami got sick, Cat prayed more earnestly than she'd ever prayed before, begging for Mami to be healed. When those prayers went unheard, Cat was angry with God. She didn't understand how a loving Heavenly Father could take the one person who'd meant everything to her. Cat had stopped praying. However, last night, a prayer had risen from her heart like the whisper of an ancient song that was imprinted in a forgotten section of her soul. Right here and now, she felt the need to pray again. She glanced around at the other patrons in the restaurant. Not wanting to draw attention to herself, she feigned looking out the window as she bowed her head and offered a silent prayer. She ended this one with, *Please forgive me for being so angry about Mami. Please help me to want to pray more often.* Moisture rose in her eyes, but she pushed it back down.

"Here you go," Harper said as she placed a steaming plate of food in front of Cat. It looked and smelled delicious. There were crispy strips of fried chicken, fluffy mashed potatoes swimming in gravy, green beans, and fragrant rolls. Cat's mouth watered as she unrolled the silverware.

"I didn't know what you wanted to drink," Harper said.

"Uh, how about a Dr. Pepper?" Caffeine would do her some good.

"Sure thing," Harper said, returning a second later with the drink.

The food was outstanding. Cat devoured every bite. When she was done, she sat back in her chair, sighing in contentment. "Thank you. That was delicious."

"You're not done yet." Harper motioned to a slim brunette who was standing behind the hostess desk. The girl walked over. "Andi, I'd like for you to meet Cat."

"Hello," Andi said with a welcoming smile.

"Would you mind getting Cat a slice of sweet potato pie?"

"You bet," she chirped as she walked briskly away to do Harper's bidding.

The words sweet potato and pie didn't seem to go together. However, Cat wasn't about to point that out. She was just super grateful for Harper's kindness. If it took eating a strange pie to show her appreciation, then so be it.

Andi returned with the pie and placed it in front of Cat. She took a small bite, her eyes rounding. "This is amazing." The velvety smooth texture was not too sweet but just right. She savored the melt-in-your-mouth goodness. "What did you say it was called?"

"It's our signature dish. Sweet Potato Pie."

Cat took another, bigger bite. "I have to admit, you had me worried with the sweet potatoes."

Harper giggled. "I guess they don't have this in Chicago."

"Not even remotely." She took three more bites in rapid succession. Before long, she'd polished off the pie. She had to fight the temptation to lick the plate. "That was delicious. Thanks. How much do I owe you?"

Harper waved a hand. "It's on the house."

Emotion welled in Cat's chest. "Are you sure?"

"Absolutely."

Cat was overwhelmed with the generosity of a stranger.

Harper drummed her fingers on the table. "Now, about that mechanic ... I have an idea." She motioned to Andi who came back over. "Can you get Frank to come out here?"

"Sure."

A few minutes later, a middle-aged man with an expansive waist and thinning hair emerged from the kitchen, wearing an apron.

"You're good with cars, Frank, aren't you?" Harper asked.

"Yeah, I'm fairly good." A large grin split his face. "You thought I was just another pretty face who can cook, didn't you, darling?"

Harper chuckled. "The Magnolia would be lost without you, Frank." She looked at Cat. "This is my friend Cat. Would you mind taking a look at her car to see what's wrong with it? It's something to do with the radiator."

"Sure. Where's your key?" Cat handed it over. Frank took off his apron and laid it across the back of a chair then went out the front door.

Cat hoped he could fix it. If so, Frank would surely charge less than an actual mechanic.

"So what's in Florida?" Harper asked.

Cat sighed. "I love to dance. My dream has always been to open my own studio and teach."

"You didn't want to teach in Chicago?"

She tensed, not wanting to go into the details of her sordid relationship with Drew. Her face was still sore and there was some slight bruising. Thankfully, she'd been able to mask it with makeup. Her dark olive complexion helped. "It's so cold there," she hedged. "I want someplace warm."

Harper looked thoughtful. "Florida fits the bill. Do you know anybody there?"

Cat's head swung back and forth. "Not a soul. I'm making a fresh start."

"Won't your family miss you?"

Cat hesitated, questioning how much she should share with Harper about her life. Then she thought, why not share about Mami? There was nothing to hide. "My mother was my only family. She died a little over a year ago. Now that I've graduated high school, there was nothing keeping me in Chicago." She thought of Drew, a shiver snaking down her spine. What would he do when he realized that she was gone? She'd not even told Romina where she was going for fear that Drew would try to strong-arm her for information. She shrugged. "That's my life in a nutshell."

"Good for you. That's exciting."

Frank came back inside. Harper turned toward him. "That was fast. What's the problem?"

He held up what looked like a railroad spike. Upon closer inspection, Cat realized it was a nail about ten inches long. "Your radiator's fine," Frank said. "The hoses are good. You know that plastic bottle on the side of your radiator? It's a reservoir for coolant, the fluid that circulates through your radiator. Someplace between here and Illinois this must have fallen off somebody's truck and went straight into your coolant reservoir."

"Wow." Harper turned to Cat. "I'm glad it got the reservoir instead of coming through your windshield."

"You need a new reservoir," Frank continued. "We can send someone over to the dealership in Montgomery and get you one. It'll cost a bit but like Harper said, you're lucky. A plastic coolant tank is a lot cheaper than a new radiator or a windshield."

"Why don't I just drive over there and get it myself?" asked Cat.

Frank shook his head. "I wouldn't recommend it. Your car would never make it that far." He tipped his head. "I think we can find someone in the next day or two who's heading that direction and can pick one up for you."

Cat pushed her hair from her forehead. Great! She was stuck!

"The Clementine Bed and Breakfast is about four blocks that way and one block up. That's the only place to stay around here," Harper said.

"Uh, I wasn't planning on paying for hotels. To tell the truth, I slept in my car last night."

Harper glanced at Frank, and then back at Cat. "Do you have any experience waiting tables?"

"No. My only job's been teaching dance classes."

"You can learn though, right?" Harper asked.

"I suppose."

"There's a bedroom upstairs where you can stay for a few nights if you want, and we have all the food you can eat. One of my girls has been out on maternity leave. It's been tough keeping customers happy during the mealtime rush. Want a short-term job? I mean, long enough to get your car fixed?"

Cat thought for a minute. It was comforting to know that she'd have a place to stay and food to eat ... at least for a few days. "Will you also throw in the cost of a radiator bottle?" She wondered if that was asking too much. To her relief, Harper stuck out her hand again for another shake.

"You've got a deal."

3

Six years later ...

The upbeat music flowing through the speakers made a pleasant duet with the lively chatter from Cat's nine to thirteen-year-old beginning jazz class. She clapped her hands. "Girls, let's go through the routine one more time before I let you go for the day." This elicited a few groans. Cat bit back a smile. She could always tell which girls had a future in dance as opposed to the ones who attended class out of a passing fancy. Today they were into dance. Next year, it would be soccer and so on. "We need to get you ready for the recital." She stopped the song that was playing and thumbed through the list to find the one that went along with the routine.

The students lined up and took their positions. When the music started, they began. "Backs straight. Hold your positions," she instructed. As they flowed through the routine, a rush of exhilaration went through Cat. She never grew tired of teaching. It was in her blood. Her gaze swept over the polished wood floors before moving up to the tall ceiling. Her studio was a converted storefront, nestled in a corner section of the square. It was hard to believe that she'd been here six years.

She'd stopped in Clementine to grab lunch that fateful day and never left. Cat would forever be grateful that her car needed repairing. Cat's temporary work for Harper had turned into a full-time job. Eventually, Harper worked out a deal with her grandfather allowing Cat to rent what was then an empty storefront Mr. Foster had acquired when the space went up for a tax auction in the 1950s. Remodeling the space was a beast, but Mr. Foster was handy and Cat was determined. The two of them made a great team. Cat's business built slowly. For six months, she lived in the small room at The Magnolia. Eventually, she rented an attached apartment from Marsha Bentley a widow in town. The dance studio was picking up business, but Cat still supplemented her income by working at The Magnolia. All in all, life was good. Much better than she could've ever dreamt. Mami would be proud.

Thankfully, Cat never heard from Drew again. Concerned that he might try and track her down, she'd stayed off social media. However, a couple years ago, she'd found it necessary to start a Facebook page for the dance studio. That's when she looked Drew up and saw that he'd married Sadie Wellington the daughter of a prominent businessman. Learning that Drew had moved on came as a huge relief to Cat. She could finally put the past behind her and move fully into the present.

"Hello, Frank," she sang as she entered the kitchen of The Magnolia the following morning.

Frank look up from the vegetables he was cutting. "There's she is … the accomplished dancer, beautiful, as always."

An appreciative smile curved her lips as she went to his side and gave him a hug and kiss on the cheek. "And you're charming, as always."

"Ah, thank you, darling," he laughed.

Frank was like the brother and father she'd never had, rolled into one. Cat reached for an apron and tied it around her waist. Next, she rolled up her sleeves and got to work on the food prep. A couple of hours later, she was laughing and talking to Frank, Harper, and Stan the other cook when it happened. Cat was carving the seed out of an avocado when the knife slipped. She felt the tear in her flesh as she yelped. Her stomach roiled when she saw the deep gash filling with blood.

"Oh, no!" Harper exclaimed, jumping into action as she grabbed paper towels and pressed them to Cat's hand. It only took a second for the paper towels to become saturated with blood. "Sam's operating today," she lamented. "We'd better get you over to the emergency room in Daphne to get some stitches."

"Go," Frank said, his voice coated with worry. He looked at Stan. "We'll hold down the fort while you're gone."

"I'll let Andi know what's going on as we go out," Harper said. Quickly, Harper wrapped a clean towel around the wound as they rushed to get to the ER.

4

Chase paused half a second, looking at the small, modest hospital in Daphne, Alabama. It was a functional, no-frills building about a decade behind in design. That was okay. Chase was simply happy for the experience. "And, so it begins," he said to himself with a grin. It felt good being assigned to an actual hospital. As he strode across the parking lot, his mind flitted through the span of time that had led him here. The first two years of medical school were brutal. The first day shock of dissecting another human being caused three of the students to drop out when they'd barely started. They lost four more over biochemistry. Having to memorize dozens of enzyme cycles was just too much for them. One more left during pharmacology and two during neuroanatomy. After that, there were one hundred and seven students remaining.

Those who survived moved into their third year rotations, which involved anywhere from one to three months in various specialties. The school at Mobile had excellent facilities, but with medical students, interns, residents, and fellows all competing for patients, it could get crowded. Students were at the bottom of the totem pole and got to perform almost no procedures. To help with that problem, the school farmed out students to area offices and hospitals that were willing to take them.

Chase was grateful for his assignment to a rural medicine rotation. He'd packed only his clothes, toiletries, and essential books. The hospital was going to put him up in a hotel so he didn't want to take everything he owned.

Once inside, he introduced himself at the emergency room desk. "Oh sure, we've been expecting you," the receptionist said. "Have a seat over there." She pointed with her pen and picked up a phone. He obediently sat on the plastic chair, a little nervously since he had no idea who'd been in that chair before him or what disease they'd brought to the ER for treatment.

Dr. Simpson the ER director came out and met him just a moment later. He was a large man with a deep voice. With outstretched hand he walked across the waiting room. In one movement he shook his new student's hand while pulling him up out of his chair. "Hello, Mr. Brooks. Welcome. Come in, come in," he ordered with a smile and a wave. He swiped his security card at the double doors and led Chase inside.

The ER was tiny compared to what they had at University Hospital. There were four beds, each in an isolation room. The equipment looked top notch. "Here's the nurses' station. You'll do your charting here." He introduced each of the nurses, who looked back suspiciously. "Over here's the procedure room. There's the supply closet. Whatever else you need, just ask the nurses for it. Come with me to the break room." They went to a small area out the back door with a rickety table. "I was in your shoes once, Mr. Brooks. But remember, you're going to be a real doctor in just a couple of years. You'll have MD after your name. This is the time for you to learn all you need to know so when the time comes, you'll be ready. You're going to work up patients by yourself and present your findings to me, after which I'll go see them with you. I'll be in house the whole time you're here, but I may not be right next to you. Don't do more than you know how to do. Don't be afraid to ask questions. Make sure the nurses know you're the boss, not them, but at the same time respect them. They've got years of experience and are a tremendous asset."

The door pushed open without a knock and a nurse stuck her head into the room. "Dr. Simpson, got a hand lac. They're checking in now."

"Put him in the procedure room." He looked at Chase. "Mr. Brooks, are you ready to check your suturing skills?"

Chase gulped, reminding himself that this is what he'd trained for. "Yes, sir," he said with more confidence than he felt.

"All right. Remember, lidocaine without epi in the fingers. Check his tetanus status. Test neurovascular function before you do anything. Don't sew up anything if there's a laceration in a tendon. Those have to go to orthopedics."

"Yes sir," he repeated.

The nurse piped up. "The laceration's a her, not a him, sir."

"Got it," Dr. Simpson answered. He slapped Chase on the shoulder. "Go get her, tiger. Oh, and another thing, that I obviously haven't impressed enough on my nurses. You're not treating a hand lac in the procedure room. You're treating a person. This person has a lacerated hand and is in the procedure room. Never treat a patient like a hand lac. They're people, not lacs."

"Absolutely. Thanks."

Chase followed the nurse out the door. Outside the procedure room he paused, taking in a deep breath. The nurse nudged him. "Time to get to work. I'll pass you things." She handed him the ER chart. He didn't even look at it.

Through the door, he could hear a woman's voice. "The next time you're cutting avocados, please remember to shell them out of their skin with a large spoon before you take the knife and start dicing them."

He pushed open the door. An attractive blonde sat on his stool facing a long-haired brunette whose back was toward him. The blonde stood and smiled. "Hi, doct—" she read his badge, "—Brooks." Her lips turned down in a frown. "You're not a doctor?"

"No, ma'am. I'm a student at the medical school in Mobile." He offered a brief smile. "But don't worry, I won't try anything I haven't been taught. My job isn't to harm anyone." He laughed at his joke, but realized he was the only one laughing. "I'm only here to help," he inserted. *Sheesh.* He sounded more nervous than a new graduate at his first job interview.

"I'm Harper Wallentine," the woman said congenially. "I own The Magnolia restaurant over in Clementine. This is my employee, Cat. Seems she tried to interrupt a squabble between a knife and an avocado."

He grinned. "It sounds like the knife won."

"Indeed," Harper quipped with a brief smile that showed she got and appreciated his humor. "We would have had my husband sew it up," Harper explained, "but he's operating today."

"Dr. Wallentine?" the nurse blurted. "We call him Dr. Dreamy. You're one lucky lady."

Harper chuckled. "Yep, that's him. I'm glad to know y'all like him."

"Probably the nicest surgeon on staff," the nurse gushed. "It's good to meet you, ma'am."

Chase bit back a smile. The nurse had a good fifteen years on Harper, but being the surgeon's wife made her a *ma'am*.

Time to get to work. Chase walked around the table and stood in front of the stretcher. He looked at the hand wrapped in the bloody kitchen towel. Wait, he wasn't treating a hand lac. He was treating a person. He looked at her face at the same time she raised her eyes to look at him.

The chart fell from his hands. "Cat?" He reached down to retrieve it. He'd lost count of the number of times he'd thought of her over the years. Her soft, expressive eyes the color of fine chocolate. Her wide smile. Her zest for life.

Her eyes widened in recognition. "Chase, is it really you?" There was a joyous note in her voice that matched his own jubilation.

"You two know each other?" Harper asked.

Cat jumped off the table and threw her good arm around his neck. "I can't believe it's you!"

She was lithe and toned. Slender yet strong. Her long hair brushed against his skin, light and teasing. He caught a whiff of her perfume that held a hint of spice. When she pulled back, he just stood there, staring. For an instant, time turned back and he was again the tongue-tied kid who had a huge crush on the feistiest girl in school. Then, he remembered that he was supposed to be the one in charge here. Even so, he couldn't stop the goofy grin from worming over his lips. "I kind of can't believe it's me either." He clutched the chart. "Wow! I thought I'd never see you again. What brings you here?"

"Well, I kind of cut my hand, and I think I need stitches," she said, a faint amusement touching her features.

He was an idiot! Of course that's why she was here. Heat blotched up his neck. "No. I mean, why are you in Alabama? And here. Of all the emergency rooms in all the hospitals in all the world, you came to this one."

"How do you two know each other?" Harper repeated.

Chase and Cat's eyes met, sending a charge of energy through Chase. He'd been so over the moon for Cat he could hardly speak two words to her without choking on his own tongue.

Cat turned to Harper. "Chase and I went to elementary school together."

A smile played on Chase's lips. "Cat was my hero. She saved me from the biggest bully in school."

A shadow crossed Cat's features. "Attempted to save you."

For a second Chase was confused by her reaction. Then it hit him. That's right. She'd ended up dating that bully. Chase never could figure out how that happened. He shook his head, breaking his mind out of the past. "How did you end up here?"

Cat chuckled. "That's a funny story. My car broke down in Clementine, twenty miles east of here. I was heading for Florida, and well, I never made it." She shrugged. "That was six years ago, and I'm still here. I live in Clementine now, and sometimes I help Harper at her restaurant. I was doing prep." She glanced down with a self-deprecating chuckle. "I got to jabbering and stabbed myself in the hand. What about you?"

"I'm halfway through med school over in Mobile. I'm doing a rural medicine rotation. This is my first day, twenty minutes into it, and you're my first patient. I haven't seen you since ..." He let the sentence lag when he saw Cat's features tighten and realized he'd overstepped. That was tactless to bring up a moment that had caused her so much pain. "Well, it's been a long time."

"Yes," she agreed with a reminiscent smile.

Harper looked at the nurse. "I don't know if you believe in fate, but if you don't, then try to explain this."

The nurse just shook her head. "I hear ya, honey."

Dr. Simpson stuck his head in the door. "How's it going, Mr. Brooks?"

Chase cleared his throat in an attempt to regain his professional control. "Sir, this is Cat Hernandez, an old friend of mine from back home. Would you mind taking over for me?" Chase could hardly concentrate with Cat here, much less treat her hand.

"Of course. Let's see what we can do." He was an amicable older doctor and clearly didn't mind that Chase asked him to pitch in. He checked the lidocaine bottle and drew it up in a syringe. "You've got to trust your nurses, but on the other hand, when the decision is as important as whether you're about to inject epinephrine or not with your lidocaine, you'd better confirm it for yourself. So how do you two know each other?"

Cat answered. "We met back in elementary school and stayed friends until Chase and his family moved across town, and Chase went to another school." She paused and Chase wondered if she would tell the rest. "Years later, Chase was the paramedic who came to my house the night my mom got sick and found out she had cancer."

Chase had sat out on the front steps with her, holding her while she cried. He'd wanted so badly to tell her that he'd had a crush on her when they were kids. Then, Drew O'Hannon showed up, and Chase realized they were together. That night was the last time he saw Cat ... until now. Was Drew still in the picture? He was surprised by the stab of jealously that went through him. He chided himself for the absurd reaction. Chase had moved on long ago.

Harper gasped. "You never told me your mother had cancer."

Cat nodded. "She died four days later," she said quietly.

A somber mood settled over the group. "I'm sorry," Dr. Simpson said. A minute later, he started to whistle as he cleaned and probed Cat's numb hand wound. "What did you say you were doing when you cut your hand?" he asked pleasantly.

"Cutting an avocado."

"Well, I don't see any avocado down in the cut. I'd say your vascular is intact." He pinched Cat's fingertips. "Can you feel this?"

"Yes, I can."

"In a few seconds you won't, but that's just because of the medicine. I can't see any sign of nerve injury. The cut doesn't go deep enough to have hit any tendons. I'm going to put in a deep layer of dissolving sutures to pull the muscle together, and then a layer of nylon stitching in the skin. The nylon will have to be taken out in a week. Can you come back so we can remove them?" He paused. "Where do you live?"

"Clementine," the nurse supplied, motioning to Harper. "This is Dr. Wallentine's wife."

A large smile filled Dr. Simpson's face. "Hello. It's a pleasure. We're grateful to have Sam on our staff. On second thought, it would be easier to just get Sam ... err, Dr. Wallentine to do it over in Clementine."

Chase's stomach dropped. He wanted an excuse to see Cat again.

Cat glanced at Chase, and he swore she could read his thoughts. "I'll come back here, if that's all right."

"I'd like that," Chase answered.

Simpson grinned without looking up. "Boy," he said, obviously addressing Chase, "you're going to be too busy working here in my emergency department to be trying to pick up patients."

Heat blasted Chase's face. He looked at Cat who wore an expression of amusement. His shoulders relaxed. "I hope you'll let me have a few minutes for a lunch break at some point," he said in a light-hearted tone, but there was some seriousness beneath the statement.

"Oh, all right," Dr. Simpson sighed, shaking his head. "When I was in residency we worked thirty-eight hours a day and were lucky to grab a couple of pretzels between patients. You young kids are getting too soft."

Chase glanced up at Cat, surprised that she was studying him. When their eyes met she immediately averted her gaze to her injured hand. He knew it was inappropriate to stare, but he couldn't take his eyes off her. The lush, dark hair flowed over her shoulders in a shimmering curtain of light. Her flawless olive skin, those deep brown eyes, full perfectly shaped lips. What would it be like to kiss those lips? To hear the sound of his name spoken as a sigh against his ear. Instantly, he felt guilty for his thoughts. Still they came, like water escaping through a cracked vase. Cat had always been a looker. But if anything, she'd grown even more beautiful now that her body had rounded out with the soft, shapely curves of womanhood.

Simpson snipped the last stitches and handed his tools to the nurse. "Dress it with some antibiotic ointment. Give her suture after-care and follow up instructions." He looked at Cat. "Is your tetanus up to date?"

"I'm not sure," she said.

"Get her a TdaP booster," he ordered the nurse. "Mr. Brooks, always cover patients with antibiotic prophylaxis after a hand repair. Cephalexin's a good choice. Hand infections can go bad really fast, and when they do, you've got to deal with a compartment syndrome on top of the injury."

"Yes, sir."

Another nurse stuck her head in the door. "Dr. Simpson, EMS is on the way with an MI. ETA two minutes."

Simpson looked up at Chase and gave an exasperated sigh. "EMS isn't bringing us an MI. EMS is bringing us a person. This person is unfortunately having a myocardial infarction." He winked. "Now you two love birds exchange numbers in those fancy phones all you youngsters have nowadays. Brooks, you get yourself out here. We're about to have work to do."

Chase wanted to shrink down to the size of a bug and crawl away, especially when he saw Cat's uncomfortable expression. It went through Chase's mind that he should've affirmed that they were only friends, but that would probably just make things even more awkward. He gave Cat an apologetic look to which she responded with a smile that said, *No worries.* Was Cat still involved with Drew O'Hannon? He'd not thought to look for a ring. Too late, her hand was now bandaged. Surely, Cat had more sense than to stay with that meathead Drew.

"Hey," Harper said as Chase and Cat exchanged numbers. "Cat's teaching an adult salsa class this Friday. You should come."

He looked at Cat whose head had jerked back, her mouth falling open slightly. "You teach dance?"

"Yes," she stammered, shooting Harper an exasperated look.

Chase was confused by Cat's reaction. Was she frustrated that Harper had invited him to come? He searched her face. "That's wonderful, right? You always danced." He caught eyes with Cat. For an instant, everything else vanished but her.

"You remembered," Cat said softly.

An unconscious smile tugged at his lips. "Of course, I remembered." Losing touch with Cat had been one of Chase's largest regrets from his childhood.

"Cat owns a studio," Harper said with a touch of pride.

"Really? That's fantastic," he said.

"So, will you come?" Harper pressed.

"Sure. I'd love to ... if it's okay with Cat." He held his breath, waiting for her response.

Cat tipped her head thoughtfully. Chase would've given anything if he could read her thoughts. "I'd love to have you," Cat answered, but Chase couldn't tell if her response was genuine or merely polite.

"All right." Harper threw a wink at Chase. "We'll see you Friday. Eight p.m. It's a date."

Cat's cheeks flushed.

"See you Friday," Chase uttered, wondering how it was that Cat could have just stepped back into his life like a beautiful whirlwind that was sure to disrupt his planned, orderly life.

5

The minute they got in the car from leaving the ER, Cat turned to Harper. "Salsa lessons? Really? I haven't taught salsa lessons to adults in over two years."

Harper laughed. "You can't let grass grow under your feet in these types of situations. When you see an opportunity, you take it."

Cat groaned. "You might as well have announced that I'm a desperate single who hasn't had a date since I left Chicago."

"Well, it's not for the lack of men asking you," Harper shot back.

It was true. There had been plenty of opportunities for Cat to go on dates since coming to Clementine. However, she hadn't been interested in any of the guys who'd pursued her. Also, Drew O'Hannon had left such a bad taste in her mouth that she wanted to make sure from here on out that the guy she ended up with would respect her. It was scary to think that she'd allowed herself to be so controlled and manipulated by Drew. Some hero he turned out to be! Her thoughts went back to the salsa lessons. "Who can we get to come to the lesson?"

They pulled out onto the highway, headed back to Clementine.

"Hmm ..." Harper said, her jaw working. "I can twist Sam's arm. The two of us will be there."

Cat rolled her eyes. "We have to have more than just two people."

"Okay, what about Frank, Stan, and their wives?"

Cat burst out laughing. "Can you imagine Frank and Stan trying to learn salsa?"

Harper giggled. "Or Stephanie and Mildred?"

Cat laughed harder, trying to picture Frank and Stan dancing with their wives.

"Maybe Andi and her boyfriend can come," Harper suggested. "We can have one of the other girls fill in for Andi in the hostess area."

"That's a good idea."

"I'll put some feelers out to see if we can round up more couples. I'll sweeten the deal with a complimentary piece of sweet potato pie to anyone who'll come."

"Great. Now you're having to bribe people with pie."

"Whatever it takes," Harper quipped in a practical tone. "So, tell me about Dr. Chase. You saved him from a bully when you were kids. What else?"

Cat shrugged. "There's not that much to tell. I had a huge crush on Chase all throughout elementary school. He used to hang out with me and my friend Miriam."

"Well, he's certainly handsome with those startling blue eyes and that strong jaw. Of course, I prefer green eyes myself," she added.

Cat grinned. "Doesn't Sam have green eyes?"

"Yes, ma'am," Harper quipped with a dreamy smile. She shook her head as if coming out of her reverie. "Okay, back to Chase. You said y'all lost touch when he moved away?"

"Yup. It was a sad day." Memories of her past overflowed, washing Cat with a sense of nostalgia."I wiled away many an afternoon daydreaming about Chase Brooks. There was a time when I wondered if he might be Hero," she mused.

"Hero? Like the Greek sandwich?" Harper laughed at her own joke.

Cat let out a long sigh. "No, smarty pants. Like a real hero. When I was in the fourth grade, I discovered notes that someone had written me. They were in the knothole of a tree in my front yard."

"Really?" Harper pulled her eyes off the road and glanced at Cat.

Cat smiled, remembering. "They were the kindest, sweetest notes. Anyway, I thought they might've been from Chase, but I later found out they were from someone else." Her eyes narrowed thinking of Drew.

"Oh. You didn't like the guy they were from?"

Cat's jaw tightened. "He was the guy who was bullying Chase."

A burst of breath left Harper's mouth. "What?"

"Yeah," Cat said tonelessly as she turned and stared unseeingly out the window.

"Okay," Harper said a few minutes later, "I can tell there's more to the story. Do tell."

Cat shifted in her seat. "Well, when I found out that Drew O'Hannon had left the notes in the knothole, I was mortified." She paused. "Then, as time went on, I started to view Drew differently. I caught glimpses of the kind, insightful person trapped inside the cocky jock persona that Drew showed to the world. Or, at least, I convinced myself that I did. Drew and I started dating when I was in high school. He was a star football player and one of the most popular guys in school. I was quiet, stayed mostly with my group of friends who were studious and nerdy like me. I was just happy that Drew noticed me. Suddenly, I was catapulted to stardom."

"Wait a minute. Is Drew the jerk you left Chicago to get away from?" Harper's voice hardened. "The one who hit you?"

"Yes." Cat had told Harper everything that happened the night she left Chicago.

"Unbelievable," Harper grunted. "Well, I'm glad you had the good sense to get rid of him."

"Me too," Cat said heartily.

Harper's voice took an upward swing. "I'll bet you never dreamt you'd run into Chase again." She chuckled. "Of all places, an ER in South Alabama. Go figure."

Cat held up her bandaged hand, flashing a sheepish grin. "All because I didn't have enough sense to use a spoon instead of a knife."

"That's true," Harper said with a laugh. "Well, it's no secret that Chase is interested in you."

The notion shot a burst of hope through Cat. "Really?" she asked casually.

"Really," Harper said with a perceptive look. "Don't play dumb. You know he is. You like him too."

A smile pulled at Cat's lips. "He is handsome." The last time she'd seen Chase, she'd been in crisis mode and hadn't given much thought to how he looked. However, today, she noticed. A little over six feet tall, he was lean with long, defined muscles. His dark hair had a messy, spiked look, which she found rather sexy in a tough and tumble way. Cat liked his easy manner and the dimple that appeared in his left cheek when he smiled. Harper was right, his bright blue eyes framed with dark lashes were his most distinguishing feature.

"It must be a sign that the two of you are meant to be together."

Cat laughed. "Down girl. We're just friends."

"At the moment," Harper chimed.

"Yes, at the moment."

The forest on each side of the road broke and they were back in Clementine. They drove through town and around the square where Harper parked in front of The Magnolia. She shut off the engine and turned to Cat. "You can take the rest of the day off. It's called Worker's Compensation."

Cat wrinkled her nose. "Nonsense. I have bills to pay and no dance classes scheduled today. You must have something I can do."

"All right," she said with an amused grin. "We'll come up with something." She held up a finger. "I know. You can run the hostess stand. That'll free up Andi to wait tables, which is where I'm staffed shortest."

The lunch shift had already wound down when they entered the restaurant. "How ya doing?" Andi asked, her expression one of concern.

"She still has her hand attached," Harper said with a dry chuckle.

"I can see that," Andi retorted. "Is everything okay?" she asked, directing her attention to Cat.

"Just a few stitches. All in all, I got pretty lucky."

"I'll say," Harper said coyly, a mischievous glint in her eyes.

Andi shook her head. "I don't get it."

Cat rolled her eyes. "It's nothing," she said nonchalantly, shooting Harper an annoyed look. Harper only laughed. "Andi, would you mind waiting tables tonight so ole gimpy hand here can hostess?"

A large smile tipped Andi's lips. "Sure, I'll be happy to." She pumped her eyebrows. "I'll enjoy making some tip money."

After the last patrons of the dinner shift trickled out, they locked the door and were putting up the chairs when Cat's phone rang. She fished it out of her pocket with her uninjured hand. When she saw the name on the caller ID, she about wet her pants. "It's Chase," she said to Harper who was standing nearby. Her heart began to pound.

"Answer it," Harper urged.

She swallowed, sliding her finger over the face of the phone. "Hello?"

"Hello," he said in a warm, mellow tone. "How's my first patient?"

"Technically, I'm Dr. Simpson's patient."

"You just had to rub that in, didn't you." His tone had a good-natured zing to it.

A smile spread over her lips. "You were there ... observing ... so I guess that counts for something."

"Ah, I did score a few brownie points then."

"A few," she sang.

"Seriously, how are you feeling?"

Cat was impressed that he was asking. "Much better," she said decisively, "thanks to two ibuprofen tablets that I took an hour ago."

He chuckled. "It'll be sore for a while."

"Thanks for the diagnosis, doc," she teased. The conversation lagged for no longer than a half a second, but to Cat, it felt like forever as her brain scrambled for something to say. "How was your first day on the job?" She wanted to tell him she was surprised and pleased to hear from him so soon. A few minutes ago, she'd felt exhausted, but now she was energized.

"Thrilling."

She smiled at his enthusiasm.

"I'm exhausted though," he continued. "I wouldn't want to do ER work like this for the rest of my life, but for the next three months it'll be fine."

Three months? He'd only be here that long? Her heart sank at the thought. It made sense. Chase said he was on rotation, but it hadn't connected in her brain until just now that he was here temporarily.

"What're you up to?"

"I'm still at work. We've just closed the restaurant. We'll be cleaning up for a while, and then heading home." Later, she would chide herself for her boldness, but the words seemed to slip out of their own accord. "Hey, you could come over if you want. We could go for a walk or something." Silence came over the line as a hard knot formed in her throat. "You're exhausted," she stammered, repeating what he'd already said. "We can do it another time." She felt her cheeks flame. *Crikey!* This was awkward! "I just thought it would be nice to get together ... as friends, for old time's sake."

"Sure, I'll come."

"You will?" she squeaked then cleared her throat. "Um, that sounds good," she added nonchalantly, silently cheering inside.

Harper threw her a large smile and gave a thumbs up.

"What was the name of the restaurant again?"

"The Magnolia in Clementine. It's a twenty minute drive from the hospital."

"Alright. See ya soon. My car's a white Ford Fusion."

"Don't worry. There won't be many cars out in this little burg. You'll stick out like a Yankee in South Alabama." She heard him laugh. "Are you sure you're not too tired to get together tonight?" She held her breath.

"I'm sure. I don't have to be at work until six o'clock tomorrow morning. I'll be fine. Maybe we can just go get an ice cream cone or something. What's showing at the theatre over there?"

"In Clementine? There's no theatre here. The Magnolia is closed. I think the Dixie Freeze is closed too. We can just go for a walk around the square or go to my house, which is nearby."

"Sounds great. I'm on my way."

"Okay. See you then. Bye."

She ended the call with a mile-wide smile.

"Well done," Harper said appraisingly. She motioned with her head. "Your shift's over. Go home and put on something nice."

As she hurried to the door, Cat said, "I hope he's still wearing his scrubs. There's nothing more irresistible than a man in scrubs."

"I'm sure Sam would agree with you," Harper said with a laugh as she shook her head and pointed. "Go."

Cat bounded out the door with a spring in her step, eager to change clothes and get back ASAP.

C at was back at The Magnolia in fifteen minutes. Together she, Andi, and Harper watched out the window. Another twenty minutes passed. Nothing.

Andi suppressed a yawn. "Well, girls, as much as I'd like to stick around and see the man in scrubs, I'd better get home before I turn into a pumpkin."

Cat nodded in understanding. It was ridiculous, getting this worked up over Chase. The two were friends in elementary school. Sure, she'd had a huge crush on him, but that was eons ago. Chase had hesitated when she asked him to come. It would be naïve of her to assume that he wanted to jump into a romantic relationship with her, just because they happened to reconnect. *Get real, Cat*, her mind screamed. For all she knew, he probably had a significant other in his life. How could a man like Chase Brooks not be attached?

When Andi left, Cat turned to Harper. "I'm sure you're tired and ready to get home to Sam. You don't have to hang out here and wait."

"Not trying to run me off, are you?" Harper asked.

"No, not at all," Cat answered quickly. "It's just that I don't want you to hang out all night, waiting for someone who may not even show up." Disappointment rose in her throat.

Harper nudged her arm. "What do you make of that?"

Cat's pulse went into high gear when Chase's car turned the corner of the square.

Harper flashed a knowing smile. "See, you can't be so quick to throw in the towel."

Cat let out a shaky laugh. "I guess you're right." She couldn't believe how nervous she was.

Frank hadn't gone home yet. He came out of the kitchen and folded his arms across his chest. "I'll check this guy out for you," he said in his gruff, paternal voice.

A wave of panic rolled over Cat, and it must've shown on her face because Harper took Frank's arm. "You'll do nothing of the sort. Get out of here and go home." She gave him a shove toward the door. He went out just as Chase was coming in. The two exchanged pleasantries. Thankfully, Frank didn't say or do anything out of the ordinary.

Cat's pulse was thrashing so hard against her ears that she felt like she could hardly breathe. She took a deep breath, willing herself to calm down.

"Hello, again," Harper said congenially when Chase entered.

"Hello," he responded cordially before his gaze settled on Cat. "Hey," he said, his tone going more intimate.

Cat ordered herself to speak. "Hey," she said, wincing slightly at how squeaky that came out.

"Are you hungry, doc?" Harper asked.

"I'm good. I grabbed something in Daphne as I left the hospital."

That explained why it took him a while to get here. "Nice scrubs," Harper observed.

"I didn't have time to change," Chase said offhandedly as he glanced down.

Cat shot Harper a look that said *pipe down*, but Harper only smiled, her eyes glittering mischief.

Chase looked around. "Nice place you've got here."

"Thank you," Harper said with a touch of pride. "You'll have to come back when we're open, and we'll make you a plate of food ... on the house."

"I'll do that," Chase said with a broad grin that showcased his dimple. Chase had always been cute, which is why Cat had such a crush on him. However, now he was very much a grown-up man. He really was strikingly handsome with his messy hair and piercing blue eyes. Not to mention the fact that he filled out those scrubs rather nicely.

"I'll lock up," Harper said. "You kids go have fun."

Cat had taken her purse home and placed her phone and house key in her pocket. Also, she'd brought a light sweater. Fall was around the corner and while the winters were ridiculously mild compared to Chicago, Cat had acclimated to the warmer temperatures. Now, she too, got cold when the temperature dropped below sixty degrees. Chase held open the door for her as they went down the steps. Tonight, the slight chill in the air was actually refreshing.

"Which direction should we go?" Chase asked.

Cat smiled. "Well, since it's a square, it really doesn't matter."

"True," Chase acknowledged, cocking his head. "Let's go this way."

Cat looked at his bare arms. "Are you cold?"

"Nah, I'm good."

She held up her yellow sweater, which was draped over her arm. "You could always wear this."

He laughed. "Thanks, but if I put that on, I'd stretch it out and ruin it. You should put it on. Here, I'll help you."

"So, you think the injured girl can't put on her own sweater?"

"Something like that." He reached for it and helped her get it on. His arm brushed against hers in the process, sending a jolt of awareness through her.

"Thanks," she murmured.

"This is a nice town square," Chase observed as they strolled past the storefronts.

Cat's eyes settled on the prominent courthouse that made up the center section of the square. Large, leafy trees were clustered around it, and a blanket of verdant grass finished off the picture. "When I first got here, I felt I was walking around in a movie set."

"Yeah, kind of like *The Truman Show*."

"Exactly."

"The question is ... does everyone watch you 24/7 like they did Truman?"

"Yes," she laughed. "They do, actually. It's a small town and people are keenly interested in one another."

He grimaced. "That must be stifling."

She thought for a minute. "Not really. I kind of like how people look after one another." She'd almost added that it helped take away the sting of losing Mami, but she didn't want to put a damper on the conversation. It felt surreal to be out here at night on the deserted square with Chase Brooks. Her cells danced with the knowledge that he was right beside her.

"So, tell me about your dance studio," he prompted.

"When we round the next corner, you'll see it on the end."

He turned to her. "It seems like you've done well for yourself."

Cat was shocked at how much his praise meant to her. "Thank you. I feel very fortunate with how things came together. You seem to be doing well too, Mr. MD."

He grinned. "Not quite yet, but I'm getting there."

"You're a far cry from the boy who cut his hair in Mrs. Steven's class." Her lips twitched as she looked at him.

"You would have to bring that up," he groaned.

"I remember it like it was yesterday. Mrs. Stevenson had to leave the room and gave everyone a direct order not to touch their scissors."

"Under no circumstance are you to touch those scissors," Chase mimicked in the whiny tone of their first-grade teacher.

"The minute she walked out of the room, you took those scissors and cut a chunk out of the front of your hair."

"Then Miriam blabbed to Mrs. Stevenson when she came back into the room." He shook his head. "I got in so much trouble for that."

"Yes, you did." She shook her head, grinning.

"It took me until the third grade to forgive Miriam for that."

"You were always the little menace," she teased.

He pulled a face. "From the way Mrs. Stevenson carried on, you would've thought I'd done something terrible like cut up my birth certificate rather than just cutting a section out of my hair."

"You got a buzz cut after that."

"Yep, my mom took me to the barbershop that afternoon."

Cat pointed. "There's my studio."

"Wow," he drawled. "You're up town." He went to the glass doors and cupped his eyes to peer inside. "It looks nice."

"Thanks," she said, feeling a burst of appreciation for Harper and Douglas Foster for helping her get set up here. Cat had always liked the inset door and large display windows. It reminded her of an old five and dime store. Also, the wooden planks beneath the front door creaked when people entered.

"I'm looking forward to taking my first salsa lesson."

Good, he was actually coming to the lesson! "I hope you're not disappointed."

He flashed a boyish grin. "No chance of that."

Her heart did a little flip as their eyes connected. "I still can't believe we're both here."

"Pretty crazy, huh?"

They continued walking. It's a good thing Cat's left hand was injured. Otherwise, she might've been tempted to reach for Chase's hand. For so long, she'd put off entering into a relationship, but now that Chase was here, she was ready to jump in full force. Was it because she felt comfortable with Chase and the history they shared? Or maybe it was simply because Chase was the whole package. At any rate, she needed to proceed cautiously. For all she knew, Chase was here merely as a friend to reminisce about the good ole days. "Tell me about your life ... after you and your family moved from the neighborhood."

"Hmm ... let's see, I'll give you the two-second version. We moved across town because my dad got a new job, and he wanted to be close to work. Also, we got a good deal on a new house."

"Makes sense."

He frowned. "It was hard though ... to leave the neighborhood and all of my friends."

She caught a trace of something in his tone, wondered—*hoped*—that she was one of the friends he'd found it hard to leave.

"After high school, I went to U of Illinois. Now, I'm here. That's about it."

"How do you like med school?"

"It's great. I mean, it's tough, but it's worth it. The more I learn the more I realize how much I don't know."

"I could've told you that," she joked.

"Hey," he protested, nudging her.

It was comforting how easily they'd slipped back into their old pattern of friendship.

"The good news is that I passed the board section exams, so I remembered at least enough to get by."

"Your modesty isn't fooling everyone. You've always been a great student." His silence was his admission that she was right. "I'm sure you'll be a great doctor." She shoved her uninjured hand into her pocket.

A teasing smile played on Chase's lips. "Well, I made it through a whole shift at the ER today and haven't killed anybody yet."

Laughter bubbled in her throat. "That's a plus."

"How about you? Tell me about your life."

"I went to high school," she said with a cheeky grin.

"I figured that."

"I got really into dance."

"Yep, I was so glad to hear that. You always loved to dance." He chuckled. "Remember how you used to line up kids on the playground? You'd make them pretend that they were your students."

An embarrassed laugh escaped her lips. "I didn't make them pretend."

"Oh, yes you did. You even tried to make me dance."

A smile stretched over her lips. "Yeah, but you were always too stubborn to cooperate." Their eyes met as a strong connection buzzed through her veins. "Are you still stubborn?"

"Oh, yeah," he said, with a surly grin, "more so than you can imagine."

"I can imagine a lot," she joked. A light breeze ruffled Cat's hair. She looked up at the sky. Clouds obscured the stars, but there was a hint of a golden moon peeking through. They were almost back to The Magnolia. Cat wasn't ready for the evening to end.

"Do you think that you'll stay here in Clementine?"

"Yeah ... maybe. I have wonderful friends. My business is growing. I feel like I'm making a contribution. That matters a lot, you know."

"Sure does."

When, they reached The Magnolia, Cat noted that all the lights in the restaurant were turned out and Harper's car was gone. It was only her and Chase. He looked around, probably looking for her car.

"How are you getting home?"

"I live close by." She pointed to a tall steeple in the distance. "Behind the church."

"That's nice to live so close to work."

"Yes, it is. I can just walk. Care to escort me home?"

"But of course, milady," he said ceremoniously with a slight bow. A second later, he turned to Cat and asked in a subdued tone, "Do you miss her?"

"Who?"

"Your mother."

Cat was surprised at how quickly emotion rose in her throat. "Only every day." A sad smile touched her lips. "It used to be every minute, but time has made things a bit easier."

He nodded. "I still think about that day when I came with the EMS crew."

She hugged her arms. "That was a rough night." She offered an appreciative smile. "I was glad that you were there."

"Me too. Your mother was a kind lady."

"Yes, she was." Silence settled between them.

"I'm sorry," Chase said. "I didn't mean to bring up a painful time for you."

"No, it's okay ... truly. Like I said, I was grateful that you were there."

"I would've stuck around longer, had Drew O'Hannon not shown up."

Cat caught the hardness in his tone. That's right. Drew had shown up later that evening. He'd made a point of kissing her full on the mouth in front of Chase, as if claiming his possession. "Dating Drew was a colossal mistake." She sloughed off the shiver than ran down her spine.

"I never could understand how the two of you ended up dating."

"That's a story for another time," she said, not wanting to tarnish the evening by dredging up old ghosts.

"So, are you dating anyone now?"

Her heart quickened its beat. "No. I've been so busy working that I haven't had much time to date." She kept her tone even. "How about you?" *Please say that you're completely free and available!*

"When I was at the U, I dated a lot of different girls."

Her stomach tightened. Of course, Chase had dated. He was handsome with a charismatic smile and those eyes. He probably had half the female population on campus after him. Something shifted in the air, and she felt a funky tension. She glanced at him to see if she'd imagined it, but his expression was too guarded to read.

He continued in a halting way, and she got the feeling he was measuring his every word. "After I got down here to Mobile, I met Amber. We've been dating on and off for two years now."

Cat's heart dropped to her feet. "Amber?" she asked weakly as she forced a smile. "That's great."

"Yeah. She's awesome. I can't wait for you to meet her."

Awesome Amber! Great! Her mind began a wild spin. She'd gotten so worked up about Chase, and all the while, he just thought of her as a friend. No wonder he'd hesitated when she invited him over for a walk. Had she not thrown in the part about them being just friends, Chase probably wouldn't have come. It occurred to Cat that she was supposed to say something. "How did you two meet?"

"At a basketball game. I tripped over Amber while I was trying to get out of the bleachers in the middle of a game. She helped me up and made me sit with her for the rest of the game. I asked her out for the next week, and before long, we were an item."

Something he'd said earlier stuck in her brain. "You said you'd dated on and off?" She waited for him to explain.

He rubbed his neck. "Yeah, things have been tricky with me in med school. Amber's heavily involved in her sorority events, and I've been so consumed with my schooling ... we broke up for a while and just recently got back together. The idea is to put off any talk about the future and just focus on the present."

Cat's white-frame cottage came into view. "Well, this is me." Her voice had a false cheerfulness. "Thanks for the walk." She held up her hand. "For everything." All she wanted to do right now was get as far away from Chase and these conflicted feelings as she could.

"Sure."

Cat's heart was heavier than a full rack of bowling balls. "You know, you don't really have to come to the salsa class on Friday."

His face fell. "You don't want me to come?"

"It's not that. I just figured you might prefer to spend time with Amber." Had that come out cutting? It sounded brittle in her own ears.

"Maybe she could come too."

This was getting worse by the minute. "Sure," she heard herself say.

He flashed a boyish grin that was so reminiscent of the Chase she'd known before that it cut through her heart. "Well, goodnight." His eyes caught hers as he reached for her uninjured hand, squeezing it. His touch sent a swift arrow of energy through her. Could Chase not feel this? The attraction ticked her off. "Good night," she clipped, removing her hand as she moved to go up her walk to the front door. When she got to the door, she turned, surprised that he was watching her.

"What?" she demanded, her brows darting together.

"I'm glad we reconnected." A sentimental smile tugged at his lips. "I've missed you."

His tender expression cut through her angst. "I missed you too," she admitted softly, and then hurried inside closing the door, her back resting against it. "Well, that was interesting," she said aloud. Without warning, a single tear slipped from her eye and dribbled down her cheek. Hastily, she wiped it away, determined to curtail any further tears. When Chase moved away from the neighborhood, Cat had cried for a week. At least this time, she'd relegated her sadness to one tear.

Cat scowled. What she needed right now was a ginormous bowl of chocolate ice cream. To heck with Chase Brooks. She'd been doing fine all these years on her own. She didn't need a man in her life to make her feel fulfilled. She had her studio, her friends, this town. Fate was cruel, giving her a glimpse of Mr. Right before cruelly snatching him away. She needed ice cream. Badly!

7

"Good morning," Harper said breezily. "How was your night?"

"I feel like I've been run over by a truck," Cat groaned as she plopped down in the chair across from Harper's desk in her office.

Harper frowned, pushing aside the stack of invoices she'd been going over. "What happened? You and Dr. Blue Eyes were getting along peachy when you skipped out for your walk."

Cat looked across the desk at the woman who was her closest friend in Clementine. Harper and Andi had drawn her into their circle of friendship, making Cat feel like they were the sisters she'd never had. Harper's expression was sympathetic, causing a gush of emotion to rise in Cat's throat. She swallowed it back down. "It started out amazing. We walked around the square and talked ... about old times. We really connected." She paused remembering the heat that had flowed through her when Chase gave her that wistful smile and squeezed her hand. "Chase walked me back to my house and asked if I was dating anyone. I'm thinking, *Awesome, things are warming up!* I told him that I'm not dating anyone and asked him the same question." She paused, looking down at clenched hands.

"Oh, no. Please tell me he isn't."

Cat swallowed the tightness in her throat, her eyes lifting to Harper's. "Yup. He's dating someone. A girl named Amber." She sucked in a deep breath. "Chase has been dating her off and on for a couple years. The two of them just recently got back together." Her eyes clouded with moisture as she blinked. "Just my luck," she said with a weak laugh.

"They've been dating on and off. That's code for the two of them have had problems."

"Yeah, Chase alluded to that. He met Amber at a college football game. He said Amber's involved with her sorority activities and that he's been so busy with med school that it caused friction or problems between them."

Harper barked out a derisive laugh. "I can imagine. A sorority girl and a med student." She wrinkled her forehead. "That sounds like a recipe for disaster."

Cat laughed, feeling a little better. "Yes, it does."

"What're you worried about? You and Chase have history together. He obviously likes you."

The comment caused a tendril of hope to shoot up in Cat's breast. "You think so?"

"Yes, I do," Harper said in such a matter of fact tone it broke apart some of the tension between Cat's shoulder blades. "Trust me, Cat, no man's gonna drive over to Clementine after the first long, stressful day of work if he's not interested in you."

"Maybe he just thinks of me as a friend." Cat's heart squeezed.

"Friends don't look at one another the way Chase looks at you," Harper said firmly.

A smile crept over Cat's lips. Something was there ... she'd felt it.

Harper grew thoughtful. "I suspect that Chase was probably thrown off guard by seeing you again so unexpectedly. Now, he's probably trying to figure out what to do, especially since he just got back together with his on and off-again girlfriend." She looked at Cat. "Girl, you've got this. You just need to outclass the competition."

Cat bit the inside of her cheek. "I dunno. Amber's a sorority girl. I get the feeling that she's probably rich and classy. And, she's got a two-year head start on me."

Harper raised an eyebrow. "Are you really giving up so easily? I thought I was looking at the tough, resilient woman who showed up in town with nothing but her car and a boxful of belongings. The one who started her own business from nothing."

"Yeah, because you and Mr. Foster helped me."

Harper waved a hand of dismissal. "We might've played a small part, but you're the one who rolled up her sleeves and got to work."

Cat felt such a deep appreciation for Harper. And, even though Harper didn't like praise, Cat knew it was well deserved. She couldn't have done anything she had, were it not for Harper. Cat's thoughts went back to Chase as she rubbed a hand across her forehead. "Why did he have to get back with his girlfriend right before we met again?" she groaned.

"Because Murphy's Law is alive and well," Harper said dryly.

"Amen!" Cat made a face. "It gets worse."

Wariness crept into Harper's eyes. "Okay," she said carefully. "What else?"

"Chase asked if he could bring his girlfriend to the salsa lesson."

"W—what?" Harper exploded, her face turning red.

Cat nodded grimly. "Yep."

Harper sat back in her seat with a heavy sigh. "Well, that makes things a bit trickier."

"Just a bit," Cat said sarcastically.

"Okay," Harper said a minute later. "Here's what we'll do. We'll find you a date for the lesson."

Cat rocked back. "A date?" She shook her head back and forth. "No, I don't want to have someone saddled to me during the lesson. I'll be teaching. I need to focus on the students. I—"

Harper held up a hand to cut her off. "Would you rather stand by like a third wheel while Chase and his girlfriend get all lovey dovey?"

"No," Cat said, her heart thudding dully in her chest. "This whole thing is ridiculous," she seethed. "I've been doing just fine without Chase Brooks!"

Harper gave her a perceptive look. "Yep, I said the same thing about Sam Wallentine. Look where that got me."

"Married to Dr. Dreamy," Cat said with a wry grin.

"Yep." Harper's eyes glowed.

In that moment, Cat envied Harper. She was happy for her friend, she really was. In her heart of hearts, Cat did want to find someone. It was lonely being on her own. Sure, she could do it ... had been doing it. But, seeing Chase again made her realize that she wanted something more. She wanted someone to share life's joys with. Chase Brooks seemed to fit the bill in every way. He always had, even when they were kids.

"Okay, back to Chase," Harper said, straightening in her seat. She looked Cat in the eye. "How much does Chase mean to you?"

She blinked several times. "I don't understand ..."

"Well, are you willing to fight for him?"

"Yes, I am," she said with a sureness that surprised her. Then, another thought assaulted her with enough force to nearly steal her breath. "I can't be that girl."

"What girl?"

"The one who breaks up a relationship." She thought of Drew O'Hannon ... how betrayed she'd felt when she realized he was running around on her.

Harper held up her hands. "As one who's been burned in the past because of infidelity, I totally get where you're coming from. However, you're not doing anything wrong. Chase is a friend that you've had since childhood. The two of you reconnected. Just tread lightly and see how things go." Her features brightened. "This is even more reason why you should bring a date to the salsa lesson."

Cat's phone buzzed. She retrieved it from her purse and went bug-eyed. "It's a text from Chase," she said breathlessly.

Amusement simmered in Harper's eyes. "Yep, he's smitten. What did he say?"

Cat read it aloud. "Thanks for last night. I'm looking forward to Friday."

A large grin spread over Harper's lips. "Alright." She rubbed her hands together. "Time to round you up a date." She pursed her lips. "Let's see ... who likes to salsa dance?"

Cat laughed. "In Clementine? The pickings will be few and far between. It was like pulling teeth to get couples to come out on a Friday night for dance lessons. That's why we discontinued the class."

"Yes, but you're forgetting one thing."

"What's that?"

"It's you we're talking about. Lots of guys would give their best coon dog to go on a date with you."

A giggle tickled Cat's throat. "You're biased."

Harper winked. "Maybe, but I don't think I'll have any trouble getting someone. Leave it to me. You just focus on making sure that you look like a million bucks Friday night."

"That might take some doing," Cat said, being one hundred percent serious. She was past due for a haircut and had no idea what to wear.

"Well, you'd better get crackin'," Harper quipped. She shooed her hand. "Alight, go. I've gotta get back to work."

Cat stood, a feeling of gratitude swelling inside her. "Thanks, Harper, for everything."

FOR A SMALL-TOWN HOSPITAL, it was surprising how busy things could get. The ER seemed to have a revolving door. Chase was grateful to be on a short break as he went to the vending machine and selected a granola bar from the options. His thoughts kept returning to Cat. He'd felt her disappointment as if it were his own when she realized that he had a girlfriend. Part of Chase had not wanted to say anything, but that wouldn't be fair to Cat or Amber. In the end, he'd forced the words out so that everything would be on the up and up. Grabbing a water from the adjacent machine, he sat down at a vacant table.

After tearing open the granola bar and taking a bite, he pulled out his phone to see if Cat had responded to his text. Nothing yet. Getting together with Cat brought back so many memories of home and growing up. Cat had always been so feisty—the kind of person who couldn't help but command attention. An image of her flashed through his mind. He smiled thinking of her long, lustrous dark hair that flowed as lively and fluid down her back as water. Her caramel skin was radiant and smooth. Her large, expressive eyes and full lips were animated and inviting. Cat was a little over 5'5" with the lean, toned build of a dancer. Her vitality and warmth drew Chase in, making him long to be around her. Chase knew he wasn't alone. Cat had always had that spark that made people want to be a part of her life. And, she didn't seem to realize how truly amazing she was, which was also very attractive.

He shook his head, feeling guilty for daydreaming about Cat. He pulled his thoughts to Amber. She was so vastly different from Cat. Amber was petite with long blonde hair, even features, and clear hazel eyes. Having grown up in a wealthy home, Amber was an upper-crust society girl who thrived on social events. Chase had initially been drawn to Amber's world because of the flurry of activity and glitz. Being with Amber was a constant thrill. She knew the best restaurants and had connections all over Mobile. While Chase still enjoyed doing all the things that initially brought him and Amber together, he was in a different place than he was two years ago. Chase wanted a deeper, more meaningful relationship. He wanted to get married and someday start a family. Chase and Amber's views about how the future would play out were vastly different, which is why they agreed to just take things day by day.

A part of Chase wondered if he should suggest to Amber that they date other people. That way, he could spend as much time with Cat as he wanted without feeling guilty. It was certainly something to consider. The smart thing to do would be to play it by ear and see how things went. He'd thrown in the bit about inviting Amber to the lesson so it would remove the absurd temptation he'd felt to take Cat in his arms and give her a long, thorough goodnight kiss. If he had, Cat probably would've slapped him. He grinned. Yep, she was saucy enough to do just that. Cat had stipulated that she was inviting Chase as *a friend* to come to Clementine. However, he could tell that she was flustered when she realized he had a girlfriend. Was Cat jealous? That was an interesting thought. One he'd have to ponder.

Okay, enough daydreaming. He called Amber. She answered just before it went to voicemail. "Hello?" She sounded out of breath.

"Hello. Where are you?"

"Out for a jog."

"Oh. How's it going?"

"Good. I'm just getting in a quick workout before showering and heading to class. How's life in the medical world?"

"Busy. I never knew there could be so many patients that need—" He stopped mid-sentence when he heard Amber's laughter. "What?"

"Rachel's here with me. She's teasing me about my new zebra yoga pants."

"I don't think I've seen those yet."

"They're new."

Chase thought Amber might ask him more about his work, but she didn't. "Hey, I have a question for you."

"Shoot."

"How would you like to do something different this Friday?"

"What?" she asked, suspiciously.

He clutched his water bottle. "I thought it might be nice to take salsa lessons."

"Huh? You want to go to a cooking class?"

"No," he chuckled. "Dance lessons."

"Oh."

There was a long pause.

"What do you think? I ran into an old friend from Chicago yesterday at the hospital. She teaches lessons in Clementine and suggested that we come."

"Yeah, I guess we could do that."

"Awesome." It would be fun to dance with Amber, and it would help him put aside this foolish notion of starting up something with his childhood crush.

"Wait a minute," Amber said. He could hear talking in the background, presumably Rachel. "Hon?"

"Yup."

"That won't work. Rachel just reminded me that we've got a social Friday night."

His stomach tightened. He was coming to loathe the constant barrage of Amber's sorority parties—the loud music, the booze, throngs of people packed into one place, people hanging all over each other.

"I'm sorry," Amber said contritely.

"We talked about this, remember? You know how I feel about those parties."

"I know, but this one's important. The big sisters are hosting this one for the new pledges."

He blew out a heavy breath. "Can we just go to the dance lesson instead? I promised my friend that we'd come."

"No!" she bristled. "I have commitments. I'm the president of membership. I need to be there. Besides, the last thing I want to do is drive all the way to a Podunk town like Clementine for some dance lesson."

He rubbed his jaw. "Maybe I should just go to the dance lesson and you to your social."

Her voice rose an octave. "Are you serious?"

"Yeah, like I said, I told my friend that I'd come. I don't want to disappoint her."

"Who's more important?" she snapped. "Some old friend from Chicago or your girlfriend?"

Amber really didn't want him to answer that right now. A tense silence gathered like dark thunderclouds, waiting to spill.

"Fine!" Amber huffed. "Go to your stupid dance lesson, and I'll go to the social alone."

Before he could say anything else, she hung up. He put down the phone, still smarting from the conversation. Amber could be so bull-headed sometimes. Whenever they attended her socials, Amber fluttered off like a butterfly chattering with her girlfriends while Chase hung out alone, trying to pretend as though he somehow fit in with all the craziness going on. His phone buzzed. He thought Amber was texting, but it was Cat.

Sounds great. See you Friday. There was a thumb's up emoji.

"Friday, it is," he said resolutely taking another bite of the granola bar.

8

When Friday evening rolled around, Cat was a bundle of nerves. She got to the studio at twenty to seven. Harper and Sam were the first to arrive.

"Thanks for coming," Cat said. She turned to Sam. "You're a good sport."

He offered a charismatic grin that made Cat understand why he was known as Dr. Dreamy. "I don't mind dancing with this lovely lady," he said, pulling Harper into his arms. She squealed when he dipped her back and planted a full kiss on her lips. It was neat to see two people who were so madly and completely in love.

"So, who's my date?" Cat asked a couple minutes later when she could get Harper by herself.

Harper wiggled her eyebrows. "You'll see," she said, eyes sparkling. "For the record, it was slim pickings since it was last minute."

"Oh, no. Who'd you get?"

"Just remember, it's not who the guy is that counts, it's what he appears to be to Chase."

"Huh?" Cat was confused.

Harper made a zipping motion across her lips before traipsing back to Sam's side.

Andi and her latest boyfriend showed up a few minutes later. Little by little, more people trickled in. Five minutes after seven, Danny Whitehead strolled in like he owned the place. When he saw Cat, his hand formed a gun. He shot it in her direction, smiling broadly.

Cat's heart dropped as she looked at Harper. Surely, Danny wasn't her date. Harper nodded in the affirmative. Danny was a pretty boy who'd peaked in high school and was still trying to live out his glory days of when he was a star football player. The man was more handsy than an octopus. *Great!* She'd have to spend the evening avoiding the advances of Danny Whitehead, and Chase wasn't even here. *Maybe he's not coming*, she thought glumly. For the past two days, she'd fretted over how she would act when Chase showed up with his girl-friend. It had not once entered her mind that he might not come at all. Maybe it was for the best. Danny went to her side and looked her up and down with open admiration as he let out a low whistle. "Ooh, doggie," he said, shaking his head. "I'm a lucky guy," he drawled.

Heat blotched up her neck, and she wanted to strangle Danny. He moved to give her a peck on the lips, but she averted her face so that his lips grazed her cheek.

He pointed. "What happened to your hand?"

"I got hit with an avocado," she said dryly.

He tipped his head. "I don't get it."

"Never mind," she said lightly as she glanced at the clock above the wall of mirrors. "Time to get started, folks," she said brightly. Anything to avoid spending any more one-on-one time with Danny than she had to.

Pepper McClain flounced in wearing a short black dress with a plunging neckline. Her hair was curled and fluffed like a poodle, and she had on black suede stilettos. She looked ridiculously out of place, like she was dressed for clubbing. Cat was shocked to see Pepper here, especially knowing the history between her and Harper. She shot Harper a questioning look and got her answer immediately.

Harper's faced was pulled into rigid lines. Word of the free lesson must've gotten to Pepper, and she jumped at the opportunity to come. Of course, she would! It was Pepper. Cat turned her attention back to the lesson. "Let's see ... does everyone have a partner?"

"I don't," Pepper said with a forlorn expression.

Danny Whitehead was standing next to Cat, as in he was obviously her partner, but his eyes were resting on Pepper. It was disgusting how he watched Pepper with a hungry glint. Cat turned to Danny. "Why don't you pair up with Pepper?"

An eager light shone in Danny's eyes as he quickly went to Pepper's side.

"But then you won't have a partner," Harper argued, her eyes throwing daggers at Danny and Pepper.

"It's okay, I can float around," Cat said. "That's better anyway." She needed to have a long talk with Harper about her date selection. Even if Chase and his girlfriend had come, Cat would rather brave it alone than have to deal with the likes of Danny Whitehead. Cat clasped her hands, getting down to business. This was her world—the place were everything was right. Even though Chase hadn't come, she felt the familiar thrill of teaching as she slipped effortlessly into the role. "All right, folks. We're gonna start by teaching you the basic salsa step, then we'll pair up with our partners. Everyone line up and face the mirror. Salsa is done in a count of three. You step forward with your left foot, transfer your weight, and then step back. Like so." She demonstrated. Left, step, together. Your arms are relaxed. They move with you rather than being placed. Let's try it together. Ready, go. One two three." Now the right foot, same thing. Right, step, together."

A rustle went through the group. Cat's heart lurched as she caught sight of Chase out of her peripheral vision. He was here alone. "Hey," he said, catching eyes with her. "Sorry, I'm late. Traffic was a beast."

He looked great in jeans and a long-sleeve blue shirt that picked up the color of his eyes. She looked behind him. "Is it just you?"

"Yep." He shrugged, a crooked grin tugging on his lips, revealing his dimple. "Just me."

"Great," she said, her heart sprouting wings. "You can be my partner."

A buoyant smile bounced over his lips as he strode her direction.

It was all Cat could do to keep her heart from pounding out of her chest. Chase was here alone. Why hadn't the girlfriend come?

Pepper interrupted. "He can switch with me." She looked at Danny. "You don't mind, do you? Especially since you and Cat are on a date."

The diva had to announce that loud and clear. Cat could've strangled her. She caught the look of surprise in Chase's eyes before his jaw tightened a fraction. He looked at Danny as if sizing him up. Cat bit back a smile. Okay, maybe she was glad Harper had chosen Danny. At least he looked the part. Now if she could just keep Danny from opening his mouth, she might be able to keep up the façade.

Danny looked befuddled like he was trying to figure out how to answer. Had Danny been blabbing about them being on a date? Obviously! How else would Pepper have known?

"I think you need to just keep the partner you have," Harper injected, giving Pepper a warning look.

"But?" Pepper protested.

Harper gave Cat an authoritative smile. "Everyone's good," she said pleasantly. "Continue."

Amusement flickered in Chase's eyes. "The lady has spoken. It looks like it's me and you, slugger."

Cat laughed, feeling deliriously happy. "Me and you, it is." Cat went through the instructions in smooth, practiced tones. All the while, however, she was keenly aware of Chase's presence. It was cute to watch him fumble through the steps. When it was time to pair up, Cat took hold of Chase's hands, ignoring the slow simmer of heat stirring in her stomach. She could tell that Chase was being careful not to squeeze her injured hand.

"You want to keep some tension in your arms," Cat instructed, "but you don't need to be too stiff. Like so. Ladies, you step back when the man steps forward. Let's all try it together ... with some music." She started the player and went back to Chase's side.

Chase's eyes sparkled with adventure. "Shall we?"

They clasped hands and began. Chase held her gaze, making her lose her concentration to the point where she actually missed a step.

He chuckled. "Careful there."

"You're throwing me off my game," she complained.

He laughed. "I'm sure I don't know what you're talking about," he said lightly, but she could tell from his smug expression that he knew exactly how much he affected her. He leaned in. "You're a beautiful dancer."

"Thanks." A smile tipped her lips. "But we're only doing the basic step."

"It doesn't matter. You move with such grace and refinement." His eyes caressed hers. "Boy, would I love to see you just go."

She could feel her cheeks flushing. *Sheesh.* Chase was messing with her head. "You're not bad yourself, doc."

He rolled his eyes. "Now, you're just being patronizing."

She giggled. It was true. His movements were jerky, awkward, but kudos to him for trying.

"You know," he mused, "if you were doing the right kind of dance, I could actually hang with you."

Her eyebrow lifted. "Oh, really."

A large grin stretched over his lips. "Yep. I'm one heck of a break dancer. You should see me do the worm."

She sniggered out a laugh, then squelched it when Pepper gave her a censuring look that bordered on snarky. Cat needed to remind herself to stay in teacher mode. Chase was a fast learner. By the end of the lesson, his steps were more fluid, and he even got the turns down. No surprise, when the class was over, Pepper and Danny left together, arm in arm.

Chase jutted his thumb. "Wasn't he your date?"

"In theory." Cat grimaced. "Good riddance." Chase gave her a questioning look but she only shook her head.

Harper and Sam approached. "Chase, I'd like for you to meet my husband."

Sam thrust out his hand. "Nice to meet you."

"Likewise, Dr. Wallentine. Your reputation proceeds you."

"Thank you," Sam said magnanimously. "How's the rotation going?"

"Never a dull moment."

They talked shop for a few minutes until Harper intervened. "You should come to The Magnolia tomorrow, and I'll feed you dinner." She looked at Cat. "You should come too."

Cat turned to Chase to get his reaction. She didn't want to seem overeager to go. Also, she had no idea why his girlfriend wasn't here, but she needed to keep reminding herself that he did, in fact, have a girlfriend.

Sam draped an arm around Harper and pulled her close. "You haven't lived until you've had Harper's cooking."

Harper blushed. "Sam, you're biased," she countered, but Cat could tell Harper ate the compliments up.

Chase grinned. "A good home-cooked meal sounds fantastic. The hospital cooks do their best, but the cooking is still hospital food no matter how you slice it."

"Smart man," Sam boomed.

Chase turned to Cat. "Will you join me?"

"Sure. Would you like to invite Amber too?" Harper gave her a look that said *Why in the heck did you bring up the girlfriend?* but Cat wanted to know why she wasn't here. She couldn't allow herself to fall for Chase if his girlfriend was still in the picture.

"Amber will be tied up with sorority events tomorrow," Chase said.

"Alrighty then, dinner for two," Harper chirped. "That can be arranged."

Cat tried to discern whether Chase was disappointed that his girl-friend was otherwise engaged, but he was too good at guarding his expressions.

"Thanks for the dance lesson," Chase said with a lopsided grin that shot warmth through the center of her chest.

"We might make a dancer out of you yet," she teased.

He gave her an appraising look. "You just might." He gave her a lingering look that made her forget her resolve to guard her heart. "I'm sure I'll need a lot more practice," he murmured.

She could get lost in those piercing blue eyes. "Anytime you're ready for private lessons, you just say the word."

"I'll keep that in mind. Goodnight, slugger," Chase said with a wink. "See you tomorrow night." With nods to Harper and Sam, he left the studio.

"Well, that was a home run," Harper observed when Chase was out of earshot.

"You'd better watch out for those new docs," Sam joked, pulling Harper closer.

"Yes, siree," Harper agreed, giving Sam an adoring look.

Cat clasped her hands tightly. "Do you think this is a good idea? Just because Chase's girlfriend had other plans this weekend doesn't mean that Chase is available."

Harper sighed. "Honey, if you can't see that Chase Brooks is into you, I suggest you buy a pair of glasses."

A begrudging smile tugged on Cat's lips. Despite her best efforts to rein in her feelings, she was excited about the prospect of having dinner with Chase tomorrow. She'd meet him away from Daphne Hospital, away from school, and away from Amber. Hopefully, this would be just the beginning.

9

Cat had three dance classes on Saturday morning and two in the late afternoon. Her last students left ten minutes after six. She sprinted across the street and through the church cemetery to her house, feeling guilty for running through a solemn place. But she needed to at least look decent for tonight. She showered and changed, refreshing her make-up and hair. Just before seven, she walked out of her house and strolled toward The Magnolia.

Cat's heart skipped a beat when Chase's car pulled up to the curb. He rolled down the passenger window. "Excuse me, Miss, but could you direct me toward the finest eating establishment in this metropolis?"

A smile stole over Cat's lips as she leaned into the window. "Why yes, sir, it's right over there."

"If you're heading that direction, I'd be honored to give you a ride." His eyes flickered over her. "You look fantastic."

Her insides turned to warm butterscotch. "Thanks."

Cat opened the door and slid in. "Right on time," she said.

"Yeah, well don't get used to it. I'm going to be a doctor, and you know we always keep people waiting. It's one of the perks of the job."

She laughed. "What are the other perks?"

"Um, let's see. I get to ask grown women how old they are, and they can't get offended."

"That's true."

"The best part is that people come in and say, 'I hurt right here.' Then I get to poke them and ask, 'Right here?' And they have to let me do it." He jabbed his index finger into her ribs.

She jumped with a yelp. "Chase Brooks, you haven't changed one bit."

A low chuckled rumbled in his throat. "Oh, I've changed. I can guarantee you that."

The way he looked at Cat caused her blood to run faster. Yes, Chase had changed. He'd filled out his lanky frame quite nicely. He was the perfect combination of manly and sophisticated. Her eyes lingered on his chiseled jaw before flickering down his neck to his Adam's apple. *Sheesh!* Even that was attractive. Tonight, he wore a deep blue, button-down shirt and black trousers. Cat was glad that she'd taken time to run home and shower.

Chase parked in front of The Magnolia. Harper welcomed them when they walked in. "Hello Doc, Cat. I have your table right over here." She led to them to a dimly lit corner table with a candle and flowers. "Here are your menus. Marie will be your server."

The setting sun cast long beams into the window, projecting a luminescent grid along the wooden floor. Chase looked around the dining room. "What a great place. I love the woodwork and big windows. They don't make buildings like this anymore. Your dance studio is awesome too."

"Thanks. It used to be a warehouse and then a store."

His eyes lit with adventure. "Let's go there after we finish. If you're lucky, I might just show you some of my break dancing moves."

"I can hardly wait," she said sarcastically.

He made a face. "Hey, don't knock it until you see it. You never know, you might even want to add some of my moves into your repertoire."

She shook her head, laughing. "I'll have to see that to believe it."

In so many ways, Chase was the same kid that she'd adored when she was young. And yet, the grownup version was even better. Being with him was beyond thrilling, and heart wrenching, because he was already taken.

Concern touched his features. "What's wrong?"

She was taken back that he was so in tune with her feelings. "I'm great." She offered a large smile, because she could tell he didn't believe her.

"Alright, if you don't wanna tell me, it's okay." He feigned being offended.

"Nope," she said lightly, "a woman has to keep some of her secrets."

He opened his menu. "All right secret woman, what do you recommend?"

"Do you like fish?"

"Do I like fish?" he repeated in an exaggerated drawl. "I've never met a fish I didn't like."

She smiled. "Alright. Then, you should try the fresh-caught Gulf swordfish. The shrimp and grits are great too."

He tipped his head, trying to decide. "Swordfish sounds good. What're you having?"

"The same thing." She held up a finger. "Oh, be sure and save room for sweet potato pie afterward."

He wrinkled his nose. "Pie made out of sweet potatoes? Gross."

Cat leaned forward, speaking in a hushed tone of mock serious-ness. "Don't ever let Harper hear you say that. It's sheer blasphemy."

There were touches of humor around his eyes and mouth. "Well, I wouldn't want to blaspheme."

She wiggled her eyebrows. "Come on, doc. What're you afraid of? Just try it. You've never had anything like it." He was so much fun to tease.

He chuckled. "'I do not like green eggs and ham. I do not like them, Sam I am.'" He sat back in his seat, giving her a speculative look. "I dunno, slugger. I was with you about the swordfish." He clucked his tongue. "Now, I don't know. You're leading me down a thorny path."

She caught the laughter brewing behind his eyes as a smile pulled at her lips. "You'll see," she sang. "You might just like green eggs and ham."

His eyes held hers. "Yes, I might."

She blinked as heat rushed to her cheeks. Why did she get the feeling he was talking about so much more than food?

"Evening folks," Marie said in a tone several notches too cheerful when she stepped up to the table. Her eyes were ripe with interest as she turned to Chase. "And who might this handsome guy be?"

Cat bit back a smile. Marie was playing it up big. "This is Chase Brooks. He's a medical student working at the hospital in Daphne."

"Nice to meet you Chase." She winked at Cat. "Better hold onto this one, he's a looker."

It was fun to watch Chase's cheeks gather color.

"You're one lucky guy," Marie continued, perching a hand on her hip. "Many a guy has set his cap for our dear Cat, but no one has ever been able to win her. You must be something special."

Now, Cat was blushing. She looked at Chase, expecting him to be mortified by Marie's comment, but instead, he wore an expression of admiration as his arresting eyes studied her. "Yes, she is," he uttered softly.

She gave him a questioning look, trying to discern his intentions, but he only smiled back with an evasive grin that was both boyish and sexy. She tried to remain steely, but a smile quivered on her lips. No wonder she'd crushed on Chase as a kid. With his spiky hair and rugged looks that boasted of prominent cheekbones, an aquiline nose, and a generous mouth, he was still as irresistible as always.

Marie licked her thumb in a swift motion and used it to flip the pages of her pad. "What can I get for you?"

"We'd both like the swordfish, please," Chase said.

"Great choice. Steamed veggies on the side?"

Chase looked at Cat for her approval before nodding.

"What do you want for your sides?" Marie asked.

Chase pursed his lips. "I'll have the hash brown casserole."

Marie looked at Cat. "How about you sweetheart, what'll you have?"

"A loaded baked potato."

Marie scribbled that down.

"With sweet potato pie for dessert," Cat added.

"I'd expect nothing else," Marie answered with a large grin.

After they'd eaten their fill of the main course, they finished off the meal with the delectable sweet potato pie. Cat relished the look of astonishment on Chase's face when he took his first bite. "What do you think?"

"It's terrible," he said straight-faced.

"You're such a liar," she taunted, wagging her finger.

Chase ate every last morsel of the pie. Cat was so stuffed from dinner that she couldn't finish hers. Chase pointed to the uneaten portion of the pie, giving her an astonished look. "You're not gonna eat that?"

She clutched her stomach. "I'm too full."

His eyes sparked with laughter. "What will Harper think?" he teased.

She stuck her tongue out at him.

A few minutes later, Harper stepped up with a bright smile. "How was dinner?"

Chase was the first to answer. "We didn't like it, but we ate it anyway." He pointed to his empty dessert plate.

Harper laughed. "You're good."

Chase motioned at Cat. "You need to talk to Cat—" he shook his head sorrowfully "—leaving all that goodness on her plate."

"Hey," Cat protested, "quit throwing me under the bus." She patted her stomach. "I'm a dancer, remember? I have to be able to fit into my leotard."

"I'd like to see you in that," Chase said.

Warmth rose in Cat's cheeks as she looked at Chase. Was he flirting with her or was he joking? She couldn't tell.

"Thank you for dinner. It really was fantastic," Chase said. "I wish you'd let me pay you for it."

Harper dismissed his comment with a wave of her hand. "Just smile and say thank you," she ordered.

"Thank you," Chase said heartily with a big grin.

"Yes," Cat added, "it was delicious ... as always."

Chase removed his napkin from his lap and placed it on the table. "Well, I guess we should get going. We're going to Cat's studio where I'm showing her a few dance moves." He pumped his eyebrows, his mouth quirking with humor.

Harper chuckled. "Oh, to be a fly on the wall." She winked. "Have fun."

As they left the restaurant and headed to the dance studio, anticipation raced through Cat's veins. She would be in the studio, alone with Chase. Even though she kept reminding her head that Chase had a girlfriend, her heart didn't seem to be getting the message. A part of her wanted to take the *all's fair in love and war* approach. If Chase was truly the guy for her, she needed to explore that possibility. Then again, he'd only now reentered her life. And, she didn't want to be a louse by stealing another girl's boyfriend. But, being with Chase didn't feel wrong. It felt righter than anything she'd experienced. There was simply no easy answer here. Maybe Chase was feeling just as conflicted as she. Or, maybe she was looking beyond the mark. Maybe Chase thought of her as just a friend. Around and around she went, always ending up right back where she started.

"It's a nice evening," Chase remarked.

A smile tugged at her lips. "So, if you can't think of anything to say, you resort to talking about the weather?"

His laughter carried lyrically across the night air. "Well, it could be worse. I could bore you stiff with long, obscure medical terms."

She wrinkled her nose. "The weather is better." She'd been so consumed with Chase's presence that she'd not noticed the weather. She took an assessment. The air was cool and crisp but not too cold. She looked up at the velvety sky sprinkled with glittering stars. "It is a nice evening," she admitted.

His face split into a wide grin. "See. The weather's a great topic."

A chuckle rose in her throat. "I stand corrected."

When they reached the studio and unlocked the door, her pulse accelerated. She stepped inside and turned on the lights. Chase came in behind her and closed the door. She turned to face him, a heightened energy building inside her like a summer storm. "Alright, Mr. Break Dancer, let's see your moves."

His eyes widened as he grinned, showcasing that adorable dimple. "I can't dance without music. You should know that, Miss Dance Instructor."

A smile tipped the corners of her lips. "Let me see if I can fix that." Her hand went to her hip. "What type of music does a person break dance to? Funk, hip-hop, soul music?"

"All of the above."

She had a subscription-based service. She typed in hip-hop. A second later, the song started as a rhythmic beat piped over the speakers. She turned to face him with an eager smile. "Put your money where your mouth is."

He rolled up his sleeves. "Here we go." He started with his arms and moved like an invisible current was running through him. It went from the top of his body to the bottom, morphing into the moonwalk.

Chase was good ... really good. Cat started clapping. "Bravo!"

He took a bow. "Thank you, madam," he said ceremoniously. "Your turn."

"Oh, no. I'm not that kind of dancer."

"Sure, you are. I'll teach you." His face creased into a lively smile so pure that it made her feel deliciously alive.

She glided over to him, feeling as though her feet hardly touched the floor.

"Okay, here you go. Start with your hand, and let the movement flow through you, like so." He was gentle, being careful not to hurt her injured hand. Cat had always been fascinated with break dancing. Also, it was nice to be the student again. She attempted to do it, but her movements looked nothing like his. He stepped behind her and placed his hands on her arm. The warmth of his fingertips flowed into her, sending tantalizing ripples down her spine. All she could think about was that he was right next to her. She looked at her reflection in the mirror, not surprised in the least to see her flushed face. She wondered if Chase could tell. He moved her arms. "That's good," he said.

Her voice hitched when she felt the tickle of his breath on her neck. Cat went through the motions of trying to learn, but she was too caught up in Chase to do much of anything.

"Let's try moonwalking," he suggested.

She looked down at her slinky heels. "Really?"

"Take them off," he suggested, his warm, rich laughter filling the space between them.

She kicked off her shoes, feeling as free and unencumbered as a teenager. She did a twirl, mirth rising in her throat. Cat was better at moonwalking, but it didn't help that her bare feet stuck to the floor. Another song came on. This one was eighties rock. By unspoken agreement, they started dancing. It was liberating to just dance, their bodies moving freely to the music. Chase caught hold of her hands and started singing along with the song. Cat joined in. Neither of them were great singers, but that didn't matter.

"You ready?" Chase asked.

"Ready for what?"

He started moving in a circle. The two of them spun, going faster and faster. Laughter bubbled up wild and free in Cat's throat. When they stopped, her head swam with dizziness. She took a step and fell. Chase went to grab her, but he also stumbled, sending them both toppling to the ground. Cat ended up with her head resting on Chase's stomach.

"Look up at the ceiling," Chase said. "It's spinning."

She looked, giggling. "I can't do it." She closed her eyes, letting her head settle back to normal. She let out a long sigh. "I haven't done that in years."

"Neither have I."

Being this close to Chase was turning her heart to a breathless jumble. She wondered if she should move away from him, but she liked his nearness. It was both thrilling and unnerving. Maybe it was her overactive imagination, but she could almost feel the hardness of his abs beneath her head.

"You have amazing hair." His voice was silky, entrancing. Tingles rippled through her body at his touch.

She got up and turned to face him. He also sat up. The air grew electric as their eyes met. She was fascinated by his eyes and how they deepened with intensity, making them look like a turbulent sea before a storm. He leaned closer, sending a surge of adrenaline through her. He was going to kiss her! Her lips parted in response. His mouth was a hair's breadth away from hers when his phone rang, breaking the spell. They both drew back, startled. Chase reached in his pocket and pulled out his phone. His eyes rounded a fraction of a second before he looked at Cat. The guilt on Chase's expression turned Cat's stomach.

"It's Amber," he said unnecessarily. He slid his finger over the face of the phone. "Hey," he said.

She nodded, her body going numb. They both rose to their feet. With heavy steps, Cat went to turn off the music.

"The dance lesson went well," Chase said. "How was the event ... I missed you too." His eyes met Cat's. A blistering anger coursed through her veins. If Amber hadn't called, Chase would've kissed her. Cat felt like a gullible idiot. Like it or not, she was playing the part of the other woman! The guilt in Chase's eyes had sliced her to pieces.

He ended the call, shoving his phone back into his pocket. "Cat," he began, raking a hand through his hair.

"Don't," she snapped, her nostrils flaring.

"What do you want me to say?"

"You don't need to say anything." A sickening humiliation burned through her gut as she glared at him.

He heaved out a heavy breath. "A few days ago, I thought my life was going a certain direction. Then, I saw you again and everything is skewed."

Her eyebrow shot up. "Skewed? Seriously?"

He spread his hands. "Bad choice of words. I'm just not sure what to do with this."

Her voice took on a razor-sharp edge as she threw her head back, eyes blazing. "Answer me this. Why did you come alone tonight?"

He rocked forward on the balls of his feet, shoving his hands into his pockets. She could feel his indecision cutting a deep chasm between them. "I asked Amber to come, but she had her sorority thing."

His comment was a punch in the gut, giving her a much-needed dose of reality. "If Amber had come, you and I wouldn't be here together. In other words, I'm an afterthought." The words rose acid in her throat.

"No, you could never be an afterthought." His expression was concerned, beseeching.

She lifted her chin. "Call me old fashioned or idealistic, but when I meet Mr. Right, I want to be top priority ... not the fallback." She hated the quiver in her voice, detested the moisture gathering in her eyes.

"Cat." His expression grew pleading. "I'm sorry, it was wrong of me to try and kiss you." He hesitated, frustration tingeing his handsome features. "Everything's just so dang confusing right now. I don't have all the answers. You only just came back into my life ..." His eyes held hers. "Can we not start where we left off? As friends?"

She grunted. "We're not kids anymore, Chase. Things are different now."

He held up a hand. "I know. I just need time—"

"You need to leave," she fired back. A part of her understood where Chase was coming from. Heck, she was confused too. Seeing Chase again had thrown her life into a tailspin. Cat didn't have the answers, but she wasn't going to be the other woman.

His face fell. "Are you really asking me to leave?" He looked crestfallen and ticked.

"It's for the best."

For a second, it looked like he might argue. "Okay," he finally said, his lips making tight slashes. He gave her a determined look. "But I'm not giving up on our friendship."

His statement sounded hollow in Cat's ears. She had enough friends. What she needed was a partner. She wanted Chase. No, not just that. She wanted Chase to want her as she wanted him. *All in or nothing.* He bridged the distance between them and peered into her eyes. "Goodnight, Cat." A wistful smile touched his lips as he fingered a tendril of her hair.

How easy it would be to throw her arms around him and pull him close. She wanted to learn the taste of his lips, to know how it would feel to be held in his arms. "Goodnight," she said hoarsely, pushing back the emotion with a superhuman effort.

With that, he walked out of her studio, not looking back.

10

The next morning, Cat received a text from Chase telling her that he'd enjoyed the dance lesson. She sat on the text for a full twenty-four hours before responding with a simple, *Thanks for coming*. They spent the next few days exchanging short, innocuous texts back and forth ... much like friends would do. With each passing day, Cat's gloom deepened. It was shocking how affected she was by Chase, which made zero sense. She'd been perfectly fine before he stepped back into her life. So what if he had a girlfriend? It wasn't like the two of them had ever been an item. She'd had a crush on Chase years ago. They were friends in elementary school. It might as well have been another lifetime. Why couldn't she just move on?

Finally, the time came to get her stitches removed. It had been a week and a half since her injury. In some ways, it felt like it was much longer. She'd begun to think of the time as before and after she reconnected with Chase. Even though Cat knew she was an idiot for doing so, she dressed up, choosing her favorite red blouse and a pair of nice jeans. It gave her a ping of satisfaction when Chase did a double take as he entered the patient room where she was waiting.

"Hey," he said softly, his gaze holding hers. "Great to see you."

"Thanks. You too." Cat tried to maintain an outwardly cool appearance despite the fact that her pulse was hammering in her ears. Why did he have to be so dang attractive? His hair was messy just like she liked it, and his gray scrubs turned his eyes a smoky royal blue. Chase's eyes were so intriguing—how they changed colors with the clothes he wore.

He shook his head slightly as if trying to get back into doctor mode. Sitting down on a stool, he rolled toward her. "How's the hand?"

"Much better."

He reached for her hand, sending a spark through her when their skin connected. She could tell from the way he blinked that he felt it too. It gave her a sense of perverse satisfaction to know that he was having a hard time with the friendship thing too. She watched as he removed the stitches in adroit, swift strokes. It didn't take long before he announced, "All done."

She flexed her hand, glad to have the stitches gone. "Thanks." The downside was that her appointment would soon be over, and she'd have to say goodbye to Chase and go back to Clementine alone, which never bothered her before. "You seem like you're getting the hang of things," she observed.

He nodded. "Thankfully, it's all coming together. It's nice to merge the book learning with practical application."

She was interested in hearing the particulars of his job. "What all have you done this week?"

"Let's see. The highlights are ... diagnosed a kid with appendicitis and had to call in the surgeon. Got to pull a great, big piece of coat hanger wire out of another kid's foot."

She winced. "Ouch."

"Hope he learned not to mow the lawn barefoot. Told a newlywed she doesn't have the stomach flu. She's just pregnant."

A giggle rose in her throat. "Oh, no."

"Set a broken leg for a skateboarder and removed your stitches. How about you? How's your week been?"

"Good ... busy."

He gave her a searching look. "That's it. I spill my guts, and that's all you have?"

"My week wasn't nearly as exciting as yours. I tried to teach preschoolers ballet." She crinkled her nose. "They were more interested in the cupcakes that one of the moms brought afterwards. We're getting ready for a recital coming up in the next few weeks." She sucked in a breath. "Yep, that's about it. Oh, I worked a few shifts at The Magnolia. Had a feuding family come in and helped them calm down. Haven't gotten fired yet."

"So, will you be teaching salsa lessons this Friday?"

"No, I'm afraid not," she said with a laugh. "I only do those once in a blue moon."

The corners of his lips fell. "That's too bad."

She looked him in the eye. "Why's that?"

He didn't skip a beat. "I was just starting to get the hang of it." He leaned in close, his eyes flickering with a streak of mischief. "Maybe I should book that private lesson we talked about."

Heat rose in her cheeks. Not sure how to answer, she just looked at him. What was Chase doing? They were supposed to be just friends. It was on the tip of her tongue to remind him of that, but no sense in beating a dead horse. "Well," she said with a false cheerfulness as she stood, "it was great seeing you again. Thank you, Mr. Brooks," she said formally, a hint of mockery in her tone. She moved to leave as he tugged on her arm. "What?" she asked in annoyance as she turned back around to face him.

"Cat," he uttered, "stop putting up walls between us."

She barked out a disbelieving laugh. "Excuse me? I'm not the one with the girlfriend." She lifted her chin. "I'm just keeping us both honest."

He made a face. "Yep, you're good at doing that."

She bristled like a cat thrown in a tub of water. "What's that supposed to mean?"

"You seem so worried about Amber that I can't help but think you're some champion of women's rights."

She gave him a scathing look. "I told you. I will not be the other woman."

He sighed in exasperation. "I never asked you to be the other woman. I only asked that you give me some time to figure things out, and you might be happy to know that I—"

Chase cut off his words and stepped back as the nurse stepped into the room. She looked back and forth between them as if realizing that she'd interrupted some sort of exchange. "Dr. Simpson's at the nurses' station. He wants to check your work."

"Sure." Chase turned to Cat. "Do you mind?"

"Not at all."

They walked out to meet up with Dr. Simpson. When he saw Cat, his face lit in recognition. "Well, hello again," he responded warmly. "It's the beauty from Clementine."

"Hello," Cat responded with a smile. She liked Dr. Simpson's bedside manner, how engaged he was with his patients. To him, they were real people instead of mere numbers. Cat could already tell that Chase would be that same kind of doctor. A pang went through her. She knew she was being excessively hard on him about the girlfriend. It wasn't Chase's fault that he'd gotten back together with Amber recently. What did Cat expect him to do? Dump Amber just because Cat had come back into his life? If the situation was reversed and Cat was with someone, she wasn't sure what she would do. Still, it was brutal to be in her spot.

"How did our boy do?"

A chuckle caught in the back of Cat's throat. "It was touch-and-go for a while, but I think he did all right." She cut her eyes at Chase.

"Well, I guess the proof is in the pudding. Let's see."

She held out her hand as he inspected it.

His glasses were perched on his nose. He peered over them, observing Cat's hand. "Hmm," he said, tilting his head.

Chase looked over his shoulder, concern sounding in his voice. "Did I miss something?"

"Nope," Dr. Simpson said with a wink at Cat. "You did great."

Letting go of Cat's hand, Dr. Simpson checked the chart rack behind the nurses' station. "There's nobody waiting right now, Chase. Why don't you show this lovely young lady around our facility?"

Chase smiled brightly. "Thanks, Doc. I think I will."

A twinkle lit Dr. Simpson's eyes. "In fact, you get done in half an hour, right? Get out of here and don't come back today. See ya in the morning."

Chase's smile widened. "Alright, see you later."

It took all of ten minutes to walk through the entire hospital, and that was only because they strolled slowly. They ended at the one and only nurses' station in the inpatient area. "So that's it." He turned to her, a flicker of hope in his eyes. "Want to grab a bite at the cafeteria?"

Did she dare? She wanted to, that's for sure. Cat glanced over Chase's shoulder. Two women at the nurses' station eyed them, their expressions envious. *It's not me that you have to be worried about,* Cat wanted to yell. *I'm merely an old friend from eons ago. He has a girlfriend!* "Sure. Hospital food sounds great," she said sarcastically.

He chuckled. "It's not The Magnolia." He held up a finger. "But the price is right. I eat for free. That even includes ice cream." The grin on his face was so reminiscent of childhood, that for a moment, she forgot she was disgruntled with him. "It's one of the perks of being a slave laborer."

She wrinkled her nose. "You don't get paid?"

"Nope, I'm still a student. Can you believe that I actually pay tuition for the privilege of being here?" A wry grin tugged at his lips. "Of course, the hospital bills in full for my services. It's a heck of a deal for them."

She shook her head. "I had no idea how that worked." They started down the hall. "They're lucky to get such a good doctor for such a good price. You're a bargain." She felt the need to defend Chase from the unfeeling system.

"Yep, that's what they tell me."

They arrived at the cafeteria. He rattled the door but it was locked. He made a face. "Looks like they don't have any service at three o'clock in the afternoon." He paused, turning to her. "I heard the Barbecue Barn down the street is pretty good. Do you want to go there or to the Waffle House?"

"Maybe I should just go." It was one thing to grab something at the hospital cafeteria but quite another to go somewhere and eat. This was feeling dangerously like a date. Being with Chase as a friend was like someone putting a deluxe sundae in front of you and telling you not to eat a bite.

His face fell. "What? You're not flaking out on me, are you?"

Her eyebrow shot up. "Do you really think your girlfriend will appreciate you going out to eat with me?"

"There you are, championing women's rights."

Irritation bubbled inside her. "Evidently, someone has to."

"I'm sure Amber is very appreciative."

She shoved him. "Stop it."

Amusement danced in his eyes. "We're friends, right?"

She wondered where this was going. "That's what you keep telling me." She was starting to hate the term *friends*.

"Okay then, friend," he countered with a smooth smile. "Let's go."

Her traitorous stomach rumbled.

"Ah," he pointed, "there you go. We need to feed you before you shrivel away to nothing. I've seen toothpicks plumper than you, woman."

She rolled her eyes. "I'm not too skinny."

He made a show of looking her up and down. "You look fine," he said nonchalantly.

Her eyebrow arched. "Fine? That's the best you can do?"

"Alright. You look fine, baby," he drawled flicking his hand like his fingers were hot. "Is that better?"

She shook her head, fighting the grin tugging at the corners of her lips. "Now, I feel like a piece of meat."

"Oh, you're definitely a piece of meat." He pumped his eyebrows. "A prime cut of filet mignon."

"Okay, wise guy. Put a sock in it," she laughed, remembering why she'd enjoyed hanging out with Chase. He always kept her laughing and there was never a dull moment.

They walked a block and a half to the small eatery and found a table. While Chase looked over the menu, she took the opportunity to study him. There were faint circles beneath his eyes, suggesting that he'd been spending too much time studying. His tanned face was indicative that he'd managed to squeeze in some time outdoors. His tan made his blue eyes really pop. She traced the lines of his prominent cheekbones, going down to his mouth. Those lips had almost touched hers. Heat blasted over her. A part of her wished that Amber hadn't called. Then, she and Chase would've kissed. She would know what it felt like to have his lips on hers. Cat wondered what would've happened between them if they had kissed. Would Chase have realized that she was the one for him and broken up with Amber? She could only dream. She soaked in the vivid color of his sapphire eyes before tracing the hard lines of his square jaw. His broad shoulders were impressive, as were his defined muscles.

Chase glanced up and caught her looking at him. "What?" he asked with a questioning grin.

"How can you be so fit when you're a medical student?"

A look of pride touched his features. "You like my muscles." He flexed his arm exaggeratedly.

Heat flamed her cheeks. "I was only making an observation. You're fit. That's commendable."

"Thank you," he said with a touch of genuineness. "Working out is my coping mechanism for dealing with stress. When I first started medical school, all I did was study 24/7. My physical health started to suffer. I was having back issues from sitting too long. Long story short, I realized that I could either take the time to work out on a regular basis, or my health would continue to suffer."

"That makes sense. Exercise is such an integral part of my profession that I've never really thought about it."

"So that's the secret behind your perfectly toned body. The constant dancing."

For a second, she thought he was joking and was getting ready to launch a witty comeback, but then she realized with a start that he was serious. "Thanks," she murmured, looking down at her menu. "So, what do you recommend?" she asked to change the subject.

"The Mama's Pancakes Breakfast is fantastic, but only if you're super hungry."

She pursed her lips. "That is tempting." Her jaw worked. "Well, since it's a waffle place, I think I'll get waffles and grits."

He grimaced. "Ugh, I don't know how you can stomach grits. You must've been in the South too long."

She laughed. "You ain't in Chicago no more. No slaw dogs, no inch-thick pizza. Instead you get grits, low-country boil and collard greens. It's good stuff and some of it's fairly healthy."

He gave her a measured look. "I'm not convinced."

"You will be when you try Harper's grits." She made a face. "Of course, it takes me a full day to work off all the cream, butter, and cheese in them."

"It looks like you're doing just fine," he uttered in appreciation. Before she could respond, Chase waved for their server to place their orders.

Cat sat back in her seat. "I don't remember much about your family."

"Well, let's see ... I have a mom and a dad."

"Hah, funny guy."

"Let me continue. I also have two brothers and one sister. Dad works in plastics research. Mom taught school for a while, and then stayed home with us kids."

Cat was eager to know everything about him. "How did you end up going to medical school in Mobile?"

He cocked his head. "You know, that's an unusual story. I worked at the fire department to pay for college. I had a scholarship, but it only covered tuition. Our medical director at the fire department went to med school at South Alabama. He sang its praises all the time. I mean that literally. We'd walk into his office, and he'd be belting out their football fight song. Anyway, he wrote me a letter of recommendation. Apparently, they really respect him because next thing I knew, I had an interview and shortly thereafter, an acceptance letter." Interest simmered in his light eyes as he studied her. "What about you? I know your mom's medical issue, at least at the end." There was a note of melancholy in his voice.

She gave him a nod letting him know she appreciated his acknowledgement of her loss.

"I know where you lived."

She saw something flash in his eyes, like he was trying to convey some sort of secret information that she couldn't quite get. Before she could question it too much, the flash was gone.

"I don't ever remember hearing anything about your dad."

She exhaled a long breath. Talking about her dad was not something she often did, because it brought back too many painful memories. She realized that she didn't mind telling Chase about her past, maybe because he was such a large part of it already. "When I was eight years old, my father was arrested for being an illegal and was deported back to Guatemala." The corners of her lips turned down. "My mom and I never heard from him again." She could tell from the shock on his face that she'd jolted him. For most Americans, illegal immigration was something they heard politicians arguing about on TV. Few people understood it up close and personal. "I didn't know how I was supposed to feel. Should I be mad because Dad forgot us? Did he get remarried and start a new family? Was he killed after he got there?" She shrugged. "I have no idea what happened to him."

He shook his head. "I'm so sorry. I had no idea."

She shrugged. "Few people knew. It's not something my mom and I broadcasted."

"I'm sure that was tough on you and your mom."

"Yes," she said simply, "it was. Mom worked two and sometimes three jobs the whole time I was growing up."

He shifted in his seat. "Forgive me for asking this, but was your mom worried about getting deported?"

"No, she's a naturalized citizen. Her parents emigrated from Guatemala when she was a young teenager. My mom was determined to carve out a life for herself. She wanted to do things the right way, so she took classes and went through the legal process. When she was seventeen, her mother—my grandmother—died of pneumonia. She worked in a refrigerated area and didn't have access to good medical care. By the time my grandfather took her to the hospital, it was too late." The horrified look on his face was touching. Cat figured that it would hit a nerve for Chase because of his profession. It was a sad story, but Cat was desensitized to it because she'd heard it all her life. "A short time later, my grandfather remarried a Guatemalan lady. They eventually moved back there, and my mother stayed."

"How did you start dancing?"

She smiled, remembering. "I've always loved dancing. According to my mom, I was dancing before I could walk. She said I'd pull myself up using the coffee table and dance. My mom scrimped and saved to pay for lessons. Once, I got a taste of it, I couldn't stop. It's in my blood."

"You used to dance to the bus stop."

"Yes, I'm surprised you remember that."

His eyes caught hers. "I remember a lot of things."

"Such as?"

A smile curved his lips. "How cute you looked in those pink jeans you used to wear."

Her eyes widened. "I can't believe you remember those."

He pointed to his temple. "A steel trap."

"Evidently," she laughed.

The server returned with their food. "Alright, let's dive in," Chase said eagerly.

The food was surprisingly good. Chase paid for the meal in cash and left a sizable tip. Cat wasn't sure if it was to impress her or if that was just his habit. It didn't matter. Either way their server was well taken care of.

The sun was surprisingly hot for this time of the year.

Chase tugged at his shirt. "If we were in Chicago right now, we'd probably be wearing jackets."

"I know."

"Hey, do you wanna see if there's a good movie showing?"

"I need to get back for a class," Cat said regretfully.

He nodded in disappointment. "Some other time, maybe?"

"I'd like that," she said with a genuine smile. Time seemed to halt in its tracks as their eyes connected. Again, Cat felt like they were about to kiss. Maybe they should just do it and get it over with.

He motioned with his head. "Well, the least I can do is walk you back to your car. What types of movies do you like? Do you prefer giant lizards that eat cities, macho men who beat up foreign spies, or mushy romance movies?"

She laughed. "Mushy romances of course, although muscle men throwing spies around does sound intriguing."

"Ah, she likes big muscles." He flexed his arm. "What do you think?"

It was impressive, no doubt about that. "Sounds like somebody's fishing for a compliment."

"You know it," he chuckled. "I have to get them where I can."

Cat was no idiot. Even back in elementary school, Chase had a long line of admirers. Now, that he was a good-looking, charismatic, up-and-coming doctor, he was sure to attract attention. The thought of her being nothing more than one of his many admirers filled her with despondency.

They reached Cat's car all too soon.

"So," Chase began, "I can't talk you into a private dance lesson this Friday?"

"I'm afraid not."

He rested his back against her car, folding his arms. "That's too bad." She thought—*hoped*—he might press the issue ... persuade her to go out with him. Instead, he shrugged his shoulders. "Okay. I guess I'll see you around ... sometime."

Her stomach tightened. "I guess so." She offered a strained smile. "Thanks for lunch."

"You betcha," he winked. "See ya around, slugger." Lightly, he pushed his fist against her arm. "Don't be a stranger."

"You either," she responded as she got in her car. Her stomach churned with disappointment as she started the engine and backed out of the parking lot. They'd not made plans to get together again.

Was this it? The juncture where they would part ways and fade into each other's memories like they had before? A smile tipped his lips as he offered a farewell wave.

She did the same, blinking to fight the assaulting tears threatening to spill.

11

Friday turned out gloomy and rainy, matching Cat's mood. She'd not heard from Chase since their lunch. Maybe she should've just agreed to teach Chase a private lesson. She missed him. Was he spending the weekend with Amber? Her imagination had conjured up all sorts of pictures of Amber. She was probably drop-dead gorgeous, insanely smart, and sophisticated. *Stop it*, she commanded herself. Her last class had ended nearly an hour ago, but she'd opted to hang out in the studio instead of going home to an empty house. Harper didn't need her to work tonight, which was a bummer. Cat was resigned to spending the evening with her own morose thoughts.

She went over to the sound system and put on one of her favorite music tracks. The music penetrated Cat's melancholy as she began to move, slowly at first with small swaying movements, and then a pirouette. She leapt through the air and began gyrating, taking up the entire studio with her dance. The music took control as she moved with a fast intensity. The beat pulsed through her like a second heart-beat. On and on and on she went, molten energy, venting her frustration. The song ended as another began. She kept going around and around the room until she collapsed into an exhausted heap in the middle of the floor.

Finally, she picked herself up. Her muscles felt stiff as she stretched them out. One minute, everything was completely normal. The next, goosebumps popped over her flesh, a feeling of foreboding trickling down her spine. She hugged her arms, glancing out the large windows at the black squares of night staring back. The rain had turned to a steady drizzle, the street out front glistening silver in the pale glow of the street-light. The street was empty, not another soul in sight. Where had that feeling come from? Were her senses heightened due to the turmoil she was experiencing over Chase's reappearance in her life? She shuddered, wondering if she was imagining things. She looked around the studio, feeling like a fish in a bowl. Anyone looking in would have a bird's eye view of her. She'd not felt this vulnerable since she first came to Clementine. Back then, she'd been so traumatized by Drew, fearing that he would come after her, that she was afraid of her own shadow. Thankfully, that fear had been in vain. As the years passed, she'd put the threat of Drew out of her mind, especially after realizing he was married.

Using the back of her arm to wipe the perspiration from her forehead, she went to turn off the music. Suddenly, she was eager to get home to the safety of her cottage. She felt vulnerable here in the studio. It was a little after eight p.m., and the square was like a ghost town. Her skin was damp from sweating, making her feel chilled. She slipped on her jacket, gathered her things, and turned off the lights. As she got to the door, she paused, not wanting to venture out alone. She pushed aside the fear with a soft grunt. It wasn't like she could stay here all night in the studio. Straightening her shoulders, she offered a silent prayer, feeling a little better.

She stepped outside, pulling her jacket closer around her. She wished the jacket had a hood. Oh, well. She'd just have to suffer through the rain. At least it was slight. She began walking, trying to appear more confident than she felt. She glanced around, not seeing anyone. The feeling of unease intensified as she quickened her steps. Her pounding pulse sprinted a descant against her feet as she hurried down the sidewalk. Her skin crawled as the empty space around her loomed large and menacing. By the time she turned onto the street her cottage was on, she was practically running. Her heart raced a mile a minute. She was almost to her house when she spotted Chase's car. She stopped in her tracks, stumbling before regaining her balance. Confusion whirled inside her. Then came the swift burst of relief so all-consuming that it brought tears to her eyes.

Chase got out of his car. "Hello," he said with a hesitant smile.

"Hey, what're you doing here?" It was all she could do to keep from bounding into his arms. She was cold to the bone. Water droplets had nested in her hair, dripping into her eyes.

He stepped up to her. Rather than answering her question, he switched gears. "Are you doing okay? You looked stressed."

"I'm good," she said with a shaky laugh. "I just got a little spooked walking home." She glanced behind her. The coast was clear. Why had she felt so threatened? She'd walked home alone countless times before and was completely fine. A thought occurred to her. "Hey, did you come straight here, or did you go to the studio first?" Maybe it was Chase who'd been watching her.

"I came straight here." Concern touched his features. "What's going on?"

She shook her head. "I'm sure it's nothing." She offered a wan smile.

"Do you mind if I come in?"

"Sure." A surge of exhilaration ran through her. Chase was here! Forget that he had a girlfriend and that she'd told herself she was better off without him. Right here and now, Cat was immensely grateful that he was here. Not only because she'd missed him terribly, but also because she was relieved to have the company. The feeling of unrest was still lingering. She went up the walk with him following close behind. It wasn't until she got to the door that she took a mental assessment of the house. Yikes! It was messy! Nothing she could do about that now. Maybe she'd just do a quick sweep and pick up the big chunks.

"Make yourself at home," she said as they moved through the

foyer into the living room. Cat's decorating style was an eclectic mix of shabby chic and pieces she'd acquired at consignment shops and discount furniture stores in Daphne. Her eye caught on the pile of clean, unfolded clothes heaped on the couch. Ugh! How embarrassing! "Hang on a sec," she said as she made a beeline into her bedroom where she deposited her things on her bed. Next, she went back to the living room, scooped up the clothes, and dumped them on her bed also. She returned to find Chase sitting on the couch. She always left the light on in the foyer so she wouldn't have to come home to a completely dark house. She went over and flipped on the overhead light as well as a nearby lamp, flooding the room with cheerful warmth that turned the beige walls to a soft butter color.

Her skin was sticky from the sweat and rain. Removing her jacket, she began fluffing her hair. She could only imagine how awful she must look right now. Her intent was to sit in the overstuffed chair across from Chase, but he patted the spot beside him. She gave him a questioning look, her hand going to her hip.

"I wanna talk to you."

His voice had an aching quality that tugged at her heart. "I'm such a mess," she protested, looking down at her workout attire. She was sure she stank.

"Cat, please, come here."

Even before her mind could decide what to do, her feet started moving toward him. She sat down a mere foot from him. Her breath hitched when he scooted close, enfolding her hands in his. A tentative smile slid over his lips, crinkling the edges of his eyes. "Cat," he began, "I never expected to see you again."

"Nor I you." The warmth of his hands felt good, seeping into her skin. Even though she was physically tired, having Chase here in her home was thrilling.

He chuckled. "I guess we have the avocado to thank for that."

"Yes," she answered quietly as she studied his rugged face, wondering where this was going.

His eyes moved over her face like he was absorbing every detail.

"You are so beautiful," he uttered. Releasing her hands, he cupped her jaw, rubbing his thumb over her skin.

Oh, how she loved hearing that. The feel of Chase touching her skin circled intoxicating tingles down her spine. She didn't want to think about tomorrow or the future. All that mattered was that Chase was here tonight. Her lips parted as she moved even closer. His lips crushed hers in an explosion of fire and emotion that ran clear to her toes. She slid her arms around his neck, her fingers threading through his hair. His strong hands moved over her back. Just when she thought being in Chase's arms couldn't get any better, he deepened the kiss, issuing a tiny moan from her throat. The kiss was long and thorough, filling her with a breathless contentment that spoke to her soul. She could do this dance every day for the rest of her life. Wait! No, she couldn't, for Chase wasn't hers to dance with. Her heart wrenched as she stiffened, disengaging her lips from his. She tried to move her body away from his, but he held her fast, searching her face with troubled eyes.

"What's wrong?"

Emotion rose thick in her throat before anger ruptured inside her, spilling out molten lava. "I told you, I won't be the other woman," she seethed. She wasn't sure how she'd expected Chase to respond to her outburst, but she was jolted to see a flicker of humor in his blue eyes. This spiked her anger to new heights. "Are you laughing at me?"

A smile played on his lips. "Carmelita Hernandez ... such a fighter."

She arched an eyebrow, giving him a look that said he'd better do some explaining ... fast.

"I broke it off with Amber."

For a second, she wondered if she'd heard him correctly. "What? You did?" Tears rose in her eyes as a large smile filled her face. "That's fantastic!"

"I figured it wasn't right to be dating one woman when I'm totally and completely enthralled with another."

Jubilant laughter rippled through her as she pulled him in for another long, drugging kiss that thrilled every inch of her body. When the kiss ended, they were both trying to catch their breath.

Chase's eyes sparkled with teasing. "You taste salty."

She winced. "I'm sorry. I probably stink too. I need a shower."

"Why don't you go get one and we'll go out?"

Excitement simmered inside her. "Really?"

"Yeah."

The corners of her mouth dropped. "The Magnolia will be closing soon ... if it hasn't already."

"That's okay, we'll go to Daphne."

"Sounds great." She touched his jaw, peering into his eyes. "You can't know what it has meant to have you in my life again. I've missed you."

"I've missed you too." His eyes gathered intensity. "Now that I've found you—*again*, I have no intention of letting you go." He wound his arms around her waist, locking his fingers.

Her hands rested on his shoulders. "You know," she began, rubbing her fingers along the ridges of his corded shoulder muscles, "I'm no Harper Wallentine by any stretch of the imagination, but I can whip us up something in the kitchen. We could stay here and watch a movie." Selfishly, she wanted to spend time with Chase in the intimate setting of her home. Also, it was nice and cozy inside. Cat didn't want to get back out in the rain, and she didn't want revisit the uneasy feeling she'd had earlier. Now that she was here with Chase, she wondered if she'd been paranoid. Probably. Clementine was such a safe area.

A large grin broke over Chase's face, revealing that adorable dimple. "You talked me into it. We'll stay here."

"I'll go and get a shower then make us something."

"Sounds like a plan." Cat hopped up off the couch and turned on the TV for Chase before gliding into her bedroom. This day was turning out infinitely better than she'd expected. Maybe dreams really did come true.

～

TWO DAYS LATER, Cat was still walking on air. After attending church, she went over to The Magnolia to visit with Harper. Cat was bursting at the seams to tell Harper the news of her and Chase. As it turned out, the news had to wait. Harper and the staff were running full speed, trying to take care of the regulars who frequented The Magnolia after Sunday services, as well as a busload of senior citizens from Nashville on their way to the beach. Andi was out sick with the stomach flu, making matters worse. Even though she wasn't scheduled to work today, Cat grabbed an apron and got to work.

Finally, when the dust settled, Cat caught up with Harper in the dining room. "So, she began, want to know what's new with me?"

Harper chuckled. "Judging by that mile-wide grin you've been sporting, I'd say things are going well with Dr. Blue Eyes."

"Yep," Cat sang. "The two of us are dating."

Harper perched a hand on her hip. "Good for you. See, you're one hot biscuit. I knew he wouldn't be able to resist you."

A giddy laugh escaped Cat's lips, making her feel like a schoolgirl. "Chase surprised me by coming into town Friday night. You'd be proud of me. I made us some French toast and omelets. The French toast was almost as crisp as yours."

"Did you use my recipe?"

"Yup," she said proudly, "sure did."

Harper gave her an appraising look. "Smart girl. Everyone knows that the way to a man's heart is through his stomach." Harper's lips pressed together as she tipped her head. "What happened with the other girl?"

"Amber?" Cat didn't want to think about Chase's ex-girlfriend, much less talk about her. She'd been so overjoyed by the news that Chase broke it off with her that she'd not thought to even question him about it.

"Yeah."

"Chase broke up with her."

"See, I knew he was a keeper. When are you going to see him again?"

"Soon, I hope. Doctor Simpson is leaving tomorrow for a week-long fishing trip to the Gulf. Poor Chase says he'll be working around the clock for several nights and days."

Harper gave her a look of sympathy. "Aw, that's too bad. That's a lot of stress and responsibility for a med student."

Cat chuckled. "Chase said he figures all the other docs are just glad they don't have to cover for Doctor Simpson. He hopes they'll back him up if he needs help, just to keep him from leaving."

A wry grin curled Harper's lips. "He's probably right."

Cat made a face. "I guess I'll have to get sick just to be able to say hello."

"Don't say that. No more cut hands."

"Yes, Mother, I'll be careful," Cat said dryly.

Harper shook her head. "Poor Andi. She sounds terrible. That stomach flu is bad stuff. Sam's seen lots of cases of it at the clinic."

"Yikes! I hope we don't get it."

Harper shuddered. "Amen."

Cat's phone buzzed. She pulled it out, a large smile filling her face.

"Is it from your man?"

"Yep, sure is," she chimed. It was a text, asking her how her day was going.

Harper waved her arm. "Go ahead and respond to him. Don't mind me. I've got some paperwork to get caught up on. Then, I'm heading home to spend some much-needed time with my patient husband who has been home alone, pining away for me."

Cat giggled. "Sam's one in a million."

"Yes, he is," Harper agreed heartily, a quiet glow settling over her face.

The old saying, *A picture is worth a thousand words* rang true. Harper and Sam were so much in love that the two of them were sickly sweet. That's what Cat wanted. And, she wanted it with Chase. Was it premature to be thinking about the future? She laughed inwardly. Of course, it was. They'd been together for less than forty-eight hours. During her growing up years, Mami always semi-teased Cat about being relentless in the pursuit of her goals. Cat had always set goals, and then worked hard to achieve them. She couldn't remember a time when she hadn't wanted to be a dancer, and she couldn't remember a time when she hadn't been enamored with Chase Brooks. His moving away from the neighborhood about broke her heart. Now that they were together, Cat had no intention of letting him go, assuming that he always wanted her as she wanted him.

Cat moved over to a vacant corner in the dining area and responded to Chase's text. She especially loved how he'd started it with *Hey, Beautiful*. Chase made her feel like she was a rare jewel. It was so different and refreshing from how Drew had treated her. Cat was so young and inexperienced with men that she had no idea what to expect from a relationship, especially since her dad was deported when she was so young. She knew now that nothing about her relationship with Drew O'Hannon had been healthy. He was controlling, demeaning, and treated her like his property. A shiver slithered down her spine. Why was she thinking about Drew? Maybe because she'd gotten freaked out Friday night? Or maybe it was because she was starting a new relationship and had nothing to compare it to except her old relationship.

It was interesting how natural it felt to be around Chase, almost as though they hadn't been apart all these years. Warmth rushed over her as she thought about their kisses Friday evening. After dinner, she and Chase had snuggled on the couch and watched a movie together. Finally, around one a.m. Chase left, saying he had to be at work the next morning at six a.m. Cat felt guilty for keeping him out so late. Yesterday, Chase had to work so they didn't get to see one another, but they spoke on the phone for over two hours last night. The conversation had flowed easily between them as they spoke of old classmates, teachers, the neighborhood, and every other thing that came to their minds.

They texted back and forth for a few minutes until Chase told her he had to go. It was just as well, the restaurant was getting busy again. Several hours later when the dinner rush was over, Cat could finally go home.

"Goodnight, guys," she said to Frank and Marie as she headed out the door. There was a chill in the air that was uncommon for this time of the year. Fall was approaching quickly. At least it wasn't raining tonight as it had been for the past two days, but it was windy. Cat hugged her arms. The streets were vacant. She walked quickly to get home. The hair on the back of her neck prickled, and she had the same feeling of being watched as before. She glanced around. No one around that she could see. Her pulse increased as she quickened her pace. She flew up her walkway, jamming her key into the door. Her heart pounded out a fast beat as she opened it and went inside, slamming the door behind her and locking it.

Her heart in her throat, she inched her way to the front window and peeked through the edge of the curtain. Was she being watched? By whom? The street in front of her house was empty. Anger rose in her breast. Was someone toying with her? Should she tell someone about this? Maybe Chief Alden or one of the deputies? What would she say? That she had a weird feeling? They would think she was paranoid. Should she tell Harper? Maybe. Then again, what could Harper do about it? Nothing. Her eyes misted. She wished that Chase was here with her.

Cat closed her eyes and offered a prayer. She was grateful for the feeling of peace that flooded her. A few minutes later, she took off her shoes and went into the kitchen to make herself a cup of hot chocolate, hoping it would warm her body and soothe her frazzled nerves. It was bound to be a long night. Morning could not come soon enough.

12

The next two weeks flew by without incident. As the days passed, Cat calmed back down into her normal routine. Well, as normal as she could get considering that she was so hyped up over Chase that she had to force herself to come back down to earth and focus on her daily life, which demanded that Cat give her dance students the valuable attention and instruction that the girls' mothers were paying good money for. It was heaven being with Chase, and when they were apart, Cat counted the hours until she'd see him again.

Cat glanced over at Chase, her gaze lingering on his strong, lean jaw. They were headed over to Montgomery to go bowling. Feeling her eyes on him, Chase took his eyes off the road and glanced at her.

"What?" he asked with a lopsided grin.

"Oh, nothing," she said nonchalantly, "just thinking about how I'm gonna kick your butt tonight."

Laughter rumbled in his throat. "Bring it on, slugger." A spark zinged through her as he reached for her hand and linked his fingers through hers. He brought her hand to her lips and planted a feather-light kiss on her skin. His lips placed a stamp of warmth on her hand.

After they paid for a lane, got their shoes, and selected their balls,

Cat lined up at the top of the alley. Chewing on her lower lip, she drew back the ball and released it. It hit the floor with a loud plunk as it wobbled along. It didn't even make it halfway down the lane before it toppled into the gutter. "Dang it," she muttered, turning back to face Chase with a sheepish grin.

"Maybe you should try bumpers," he teased after Cat's second ball went into the gutter.

Chase lined up and threw his ball. It went straight down the center and knocked down all the pins except for one on the far left.

"Wow, you're good."

He just grinned. He aimed for the left pin and almost made it, but the ball went into the gutter right before it made contact with the pin. He slapped his thigh, shaking his head.

"Better luck next time," she called.

Her second time around, Cat knocked down all but two pins. She could tell that Chase was impressed. Even more so when she took out the remaining pins. She jumped into the air with a whoop. She spun around without realizing how close Chase was behind her as she fell into his arms.

His light eyes sparkled as he caught her around the waist and pulled her close. "Congratulations, slugger."

"Thank you." His body was solid, well-muscled, and warm. He smelled amazing. For a second, she lost her train of thought as she gazed googly eyed at him. She could tell from the quirky look on his face that he knew the effect he had on her. He gave her a peck on the lips that shot tingles through her. "We'll have to pick this up later," he murmured in her ear.

Yes, please! She went over to the chairs and sat down while Chase picked up his bowling ball and set his stance. Sheesh, those jeans looked good on his long muscular legs. He reared back and let loose a stunning gutter ball.

"That was a waste of a spare," he lamented as he picked up the ball and tossed it again, knocking down half the pins. Before the game was over, Chase got three strikes and several more spares. Clearly, Cat was not going to win this game. Then again, she was the real winner where it counted the most because she'd gotten Chase.

They played another round before grabbing a pizza at the café inside the bowling alley. Chase had kept her laughing all night with his witty comments. She liked how comfortable he was in his own skin, not the kind of guy who needed his ego stroked. After one of his strikes, he'd moonwalked across the top of the lane, earning applause from the people around them. Cat enjoyed listening to his stories of people who came into the emergency room.

"I couldn't believe it," he said. "So we admitted the guy, did his upper endoscopy to see why he was throwing up blood, cauterized his bleeding ulcer, and put him to bed. He was on a strict no-food order. He had a nasogastric tube in place, sucking all the stomach acid out of him so his ulcer could heal, but it wouldn't heal. He kept complaining of pain, and we kept seeing blood come up his tube. On his fourth day in the hospital, we were about to take him to surgery and cut him open to try and figure out why he wasn't healing. I kicked something under his bed. When I squatted down to see what it was, I found a gallon-sized jar of pickled jalapeños that his family had snuck in." He threw up his hands, showing that adorable dimple. "No wonder his ulcers wouldn't heal."

Cat laughed so hard she was afraid her drink was going to come out her nose. "I can't believe that." She shook her head. "Did it ever occur to them that they were working against you?"

"Apparently not. To them, we were just the mean doctors starving Grandpa."

She giggled. "Tell me another one."

"Okay. We had a lady come in with horrible lower stomach pains. Everyone had always assumed her irregular cycles were because of her size. We did blood tests, examined her and re-examined her. We called in the surgery residents for their opinion, but they were no help and signed off of her case. The GI fellows had no clue what was going on. We called urology since nobody else had found anything. They ordered a CT scan, and just as the radiology transport was about to wheel her out of the ER, her pains shot through the roof. I mean, she woke up everybody with her screaming. Long story short, three hours later we sent her home with her healthy nine-pound baby boy."

Her eyes lassoed to large circles. "What? She didn't know she was pregnant?"

"Nope. She had no clue. I'd heard stories like that back in my fire-fighter days, but I've never been part of one until I got here."

Cat shook her head. "That's crazy."

A grin tugged at his lips. "Yeah, but it sure keeps things interesting. Are you done eating?" Half the pizza was left.

Cat clutched her stomach. "I'm stuffed. We should get a to-go box for you to take it with you. I get all the food I can eat at The Magnolia."

"And I get everything free at the hospital cafeteria."

"Oh, yeah. That's right. Lucky you."

"It's full of fat and salt and not good for hospital patients or any of the rest of us, but it's free. I won't turn down pizza though. It'll make a good midnight snack."

After grabbing a pizza box, they headed out. Chase put his hand in the small of her back as they walked. Cat liked the feel of his easy touch and how protected she felt with him. Life was so much more thrilling with Chase back in her life.

When they got into the car, Chase turned on the radio and began singing along. Cat leaned across the console and rested her head on his arm. The rhythmic beat of tires on the highway lulled her to sleep. Before she knew it, they were back in Clementine. "I'm sorry I fell asleep," she said with a yawn.

"No worries. You were cute snoring."

She blinked. "I was not snoring, was I?" *How embarrassing!*

He pushed out a triumphant laugh. "Gotcha."

She shoved him, shaking her head. "You wanna come in?" Tingles circled through her thinking of the goodnight kiss, which was sure to come shortly.

He glanced at the clock on his dash. "I can't stay long because I have an early morning at the hospital, but I can stay for a few minutes."

They walked hand-in-hand to the door. Cat fished in her purse for the key to open the door. Chase touched the doorknob. "It's unlocked."

She froze. "What?"

Chase turned the doorknob to demonstrate, pushing open the door.

Shivers ran down her spine. "That's strange."

They stepped inside. Cat's insides knotted as she looked around.

"Do you think you just forgot to lock it?" Chase asked, noting her concern.

"Maybe." Cat tried to think. She'd rushed home from the studio and showered. Shortly thereafter, Chase had picked her up. She honestly couldn't remember if she'd locked the door.

"Let's do a check of the house," Chase suggested.

"Good idea." Had Chase not been here with her, Cat would've been freaking out. Chase stayed by her side as they went methodically room by room. Everything appeared to be in order. The tension inside Cat ebbed as her shoulders relaxed. She offered Chase an apologetic grin. "I probably did just forget to lock it." She didn't have an alarm system on her home. In Clementine, it hardly seemed necessary. Also, it was an extra expense. Now, however, she wondered if she should consider it.

Chase took her hand and led her over to the couch. "So," he began with a teasing glimmer in his eyes. "What was all that talk about you kicking my butt in bowling?"

Laughter flowed up from her throat, dispelling the last of her unease. "Hey, now, don't rub it in."

"Oh, I wouldn't dream of it—" he winked "—much."

"I see how it is," she drawled.

His gaze moved over her, the smolder in his cobalt eyes caused her blood to run faster. He touched her hair, wrapping a finger around a curl. "You have the most fascinating hair. I can't decide if I like it better curly or straight."

She smiled. "For me, it depends on the day." Normally, she blew her hair out straight, but today, she'd let it do its thing. His hand moved to her cheek as he traced a pattern along the edge of her jaw with deliberate lightness that stirred warm ribbons of desire through her stomach. Her lips parted in acceptance as his mouth took hers. The kiss was surprisingly gentle. Her mind got wrapped in the velvety warmth of his lips as she melted into him. She was the one who deepened it as a flame raced through her. She pressed her lips to his with a hungry urgency that sent them both tumbling into waves of euphoria.

When they pulled away, a smile tipped Chase's lips. "You are amazing. Carmelita Hernandez, I'm falling hard for you."

Happiness bubbled in her chest. "That's nice to know," she quipped.

He raised an eyebrow. "Really?"

Her lips twitched with amusement at seeing his put-out expression. "Yes, because I'm falling for you too." *It's always been you,* her mind added. Maybe her Mami was right. Cat had set her heart on Chase Brooks long ago before she even fully understood what love between a man and woman really was. Even so, her childhood insight was proving to be right on track. Chase was everything and more that she'd ever hoped for.

After a few more slow, shivery kisses that left her body quivering, Chase remorsefully announced that he needed to go. Cat walked him to the door and watched as he strode down the walk in long, fluid strides. When he got to his car, he turned giving her an adventurous grin that caused her heart to turn over. Offering a farewell wave, she closed the door. This time, she made a point of locking it before heading off to bed.

As she drifted off to sleep, her mind kept returning to the unlocked door. In the end, she figured she probably had just forgotten to lock it. If someone had come in, there would be some evidence of it, right? Everything had seemed perfectly normal. Just before sleep overtook her, she vowed to be more careful in the future.

Yes, it was Clementine, probably one of the safest places on earth. Still, one could never be too cautious.

THE NEXT FEW days passed so quickly that Cat felt like it was a blur. Chase worked a lot of shifts, making sure to check in with her every chance he got. With the approaching recital, things at the studio were ramping into high gear. Cat ran through her mental list of the performances. There would be five groups of kids in all, ranging from toddlers to high schoolers. She needed to spend some time working with the high school group on their hip-hop performance. Also, the middle schoolers were doing a classical European dance number that needed more work. The audience wouldn't expect much from the younger dancers, but the older ones needed to shine. Normally, the weeks before the recital were all-consuming. This time, however, Dr. Blue Eyes was stealing away the bulk of her attention. She grinned thinking of Chase. She'd not heard from him today. He was probably too busy at work.

The two of them were getting together this evening for a late dinner. Cat was making Chase one of Mami's Guatemalan dishes. Finding a Mexican grocery had been the trickiest part. Harper had tracked one down for her online. Yesterday, after the last dance class was over, Cat had darted over to Daphne and picked up the ingredients, which included coriander, achiote, and chilis. She'd been tempted to stop by the hospital to see Chase but didn't want to be a nuisance, especially since he was always so busy during his shifts.

Her last class ended at seven tonight. Chase didn't get off until eight. Hopefully, by the time he arrived, Cat would have the bulk of the meal prepared. Her mouth watered thinking of the flaky empanadas stuffed with pork and veggies. She'd pair that with kak'ik, a spicy stew garnished with cilantro, lime, avocado, and a bowl of chile paste on the side. For dessert, there would be rellenitos made from plantain dough and stuffed with custard and topped with a black bean sauce.

Planning this meal had turned Cat's thoughts to Mami, making Cat miss her even more than usual. Cat could only imagine how surprised Mami would be to learn that Cat and Chase were together. Mami had known about her crush on Chase and had labeled him as a *Nice Boy*.

Cat's four-thirty class with ten and eleven-year-olds had just ended. The upbeat murmurs of conversation between her students and the moms waiting in the foyer bubbled through the studio. "Be sure and practice the routine," Cat encouraged loud enough for the moms to hear. "You want to be ready for the recital."

"Yes, Miss Hernandez," a few of the girls said dutifully in singsong voices as they skipped away. Cat smiled, figuring that all thoughts of dance would flee out of their heads, probably before they even left the studio. As the girls filed out with their moms, Cat felt eyes on her, realized a woman was staring or scrutinizing her. The woman was stunningly beautiful with a mane of flame-red hair that framed her porcelain features in soft waves. She was dressed to the nines and didn't appear to be interested in talking to any of the moms. There was an air of haughtiness about the woman that was off-putting. Cat felt the woman's hostility from across the room.

The woman stood and approached Cat. She had a petite build, but with her tall heels, she and Cat were eye level.

"May I help you?" Cat asked, lifting her chin.

A sneer twisted over the woman's face. "Did you really think you were just gonna waltz in and steal him from me?"

The comment came at Cat like a punch in the gut as she rocked back. "I beg your pardon." She looked past the woman to the last mom and girl who'd walked out the door. *Great!* Now they were alone.

A derisive chortle rose in the redhead's throat. "You don't have what it takes to hold onto Chase."

Cat's brain connected the dots. "You're Amber."

"Chase is not with you because he cares." Amber's husky, cultured voice slithered around Cat like a python encircling its prey. "He feels sorry for you." Her full lips formed a pout. "The poor illegal whose dad was deported." Rage twisted her face. "People like you are disgusting, leeching off this country's resources."

The blood drained from Cat's face, trembles running through her body. "I'm an American, same as you."

Amber gave her a withering look. "There's nothing the same about me and you."

Had Chase told Amber about her dad getting deported? Why would he do that? The acerbic sting of betrayal rose in her throat. Did Chase feel sorry for her? She'd trusted him ... told him about her past, never dreaming that he'd go blabbing it to Amber.

"Do you have any idea what Chase is giving up for you? Do you," she hissed, getting up in Cat's face.

Cat was sure that given time, there was plenty she could think to say to this devil debutante. At the moment, however, her words were frozen. All she could do was gape. She'd thought Amber beautiful at first glance, but the woman's inner ugliness overshadowed all else. Her face was an ugly tomato red, matching her hair.

"Thanks to my father, Chase was guaranteed a position at the pediatric unit at St. Mark's Hospital in Jacksonville, Florida, when he finishes his schooling." Her voice escalated. "Do you know how rare it is to get a position like that? Do you?" she screamed.

Cat found her voice. "Chase doesn't even know what area he wants to specialize in yet. How could he possibly have his future planned out?"

Amber barked out a sneer. "You don't know anything." The coldness of her words cut through Cat like a frigid blast. Amber looked her up and down, malice glittering in her jade eyes. "Let me tell you how this is gonna go, chica."

Chica? Seriously? The condescension in Amber's tone was astounding.

"Chase's little trip down memory lane is officially over," Amber continued. "He'll come to his senses and realize that he was duped by a second-rate floozy who's been catting around behind his back. And when he does, his long-suffering, patient girlfriend will be there to pick up the pieces." She threw back her head, giving her hair a flick.

"You've done me a favor, actually." She chuckled. "Now, Chase will be beholden to me for the long haul."

The hair on Cat's neck rose. Catting around? Was Amber delusional? This was absurd! "I don't know who you think you are, but you've got less than twenty seconds to get out of my studio before I wipe that neon-red lipstick off your spiteful lips." The only thing that kept Cat from socking the woman in the jaw was the knowledge that it would cause her more problems on the backend than it was worth. No doubt Amber would go after Cat for assault. That's probably what she was doing—baiting Cat so she would attack. "Get out!" Cat demanded.

A scornful smile twisted over Amber's lips. "Sure thing, chica. Just one more thing—I'll win," she taunted, her eyes glittering with confidence. "I always do." With that, she turned on her heel and strutted out.

Cat's pulse was thrashing against her ears. The anger was so blistering hot that it nearly choked off her breath. Amber's hateful words ran through her mind, stopping at the part where she talked about the deportation. Chase had to have told Amber that. Otherwise, how would she have known? Tears rose in her eyes, nausea churning her gut. The students for her six o'clock class began arriving. Cat glanced at the clock on the wall. She still had twelve minutes until the class started. Her wrath was burning a hole through her. She grabbed her phone and went to the restroom in the back. She stepped in and closed the door, dialing Chase. It went to voicemail.

"How could you?" she began. "The things I told you about my dad being deported were private. You had no right to tell Amber." Her voice quivered, her air getting cut off as she began again. "Amber had no right to come here and threaten me. I don't know what game you're playing, but it's over!" A tidal wave of emotion rose in her throat as she swallowed. "Don't ever come near me again!" She ended the call, her hands shaking profusely. Tears welled in her eyes, dribbling down her cheeks. A sob rose in her chest. She gulped it back down, knowing she couldn't give in to the grief. She had students waiting, a class to teach. She leaned against the door, attempting to pull herself together. A fierce headache pounded against the bridge of her nose. She wanted to go home and forget this day ever happened. An image of Chase flashed through her mind, gutting her insides. She'd been so happy, so hopeful for the future. Now, in one fell swoop, everything had imploded. She sucked in a ragged breath, determined to stay the emotion. She had the rest of her life to fall apart, but for the next hour, she had to hold it together.

A few minutes later, she emerged from the restroom. Her posture was stiff, her chin held high as she went to greet her students. Only one thought kept running through her mind—how could she have been so wrong about Chase?

13

Finally! The class was over. Cat had managed to get through it with only one student asking her if she was okay. She'd plastered on a large smile and answered with a resounding, *Of course*. After the last student left, she gathered her things and headed for home. She'd missed several calls from Chase, but he hadn't left a message. It was just as well. There was nothing he could say to fix the situation. He'd betrayed her trust, told Amber private things about her, things that Amber had used as a weapon. Her anger from earlier subsided to a numbing ache that permeated every inch of her body. She wanted to fall into the bed and sleep for a week. She thought of the ingredients that she'd so painstakingly gathered for tonight's dinner. Chase had seemed excited about her cooking some of Mami's dishes. Now, her effort seemed foolish and naïve.

There was a light breeze in the air that ruffled Cat's clothes. She looked up at the evening sky, which had deepened to an inky indigo. A bright yellow moon shone overhead. It was a perfect evening—not too hot, not too cold. The irony was not lost on Cat. Tonight would've been perfect for a moonlight stroll with Chase. She looked at the moon again, scowling. She felt like it was jeering at her misfortune. She was about to go up the walk leading to her house when a flash of white caught her eye. She halted in her tracks, her pulse ratcheting up. At the foot of the large, leafy tree bordering the edge of her yard was a white slip of paper weighted down by a rock. She glanced around before going over to it. Had it been here this morning? With trembling hands, she slid the paper out from underneath the rock. It was folded into a neat square. Swallowing, she opened it, dreading what she would find inside. She exhaled a relieved breath when she saw that it was blank. Had a child left it? Perhaps. She looked around again, seeing no one. Taking in a deep breath, she walked across the yard to her front door. What a day this had been!

For good measure, she tried the front door before she thrust in her key. It was locked, just as she'd left it. She unlocked the door and went inside. She went to the kitchen and deposited her things on the table. She'd just turned on the kitchen light when a movement from behind caught her attention. She whirled around, coming face to face with the one person she'd hoped never to see again.

"Hello, Cat. Did you miss me?"

Terror slammed against her ribcage as she shrank back against the wall. "D—drew?" she stammered. "What're you doing here?" He was an imposing mountain with his large, muscular stature. His blonde hair was receding, his jaw was collecting flesh, and his face was more lined than she remembered. Her gaze settled on his cold, calculating eyes. Same old Drew. She thought of her purse on the table. If she could just get to her phone ...

Drew seemed to be reading her thoughts. He clicked his tongue in amusement, shaking his head back and forth. "Don't even try it."

"You broke into my house," she said, stating the obvious.

"On several occasions."

A chill ran down her spine. She thought of the unlocked door, the feeling of being watched. Anger coursed through her veins as her eyes narrowed. "Does your wife know you're here?"

He barked out a laugh. "I doubt that she'd care much," he said casually, "considering that she's taking me for every penny I've got." He darted forward, clutching Cat's arm.

She yelped. "What're you doing?" His fingers were digging into her flesh.

"It's time the two of us had a nice, long chat." His ruthless expression chilled her to the bone. Drew was dangerous. She shuddered to think of what evil plan he'd concocted in his brain.

He dragged her over to the kitchen table and shoved her into a chair. Then, with a swipe of his arm, he sent her purse, file folder full of papers, and jacket flying off the table. He pulled back a chair with a loud scrape and sat down.

His eyes raked over her boldly with no shame. "You're still beautiful." Her stomach roiled when she saw the glimmer of lust. "Do you know how long I looked for you?" His eyes hardened. "Do you?" he yelled, pounding the table, causing her to flinch. "You left without so much as a word," he mused reaching over and rubbing a finger over her jaw.

She backed away, grunting in disgust. "I left because I was done with you and your pathetic antics. You can't bully someone into having a relationship with you, Drew."

He caught her hair in his fist, yanking her towards him. "Don't ever talk to me like that again," he seethed.

"You're hurting me, Drew," she squeaked, terror clawing her insides.

He released her hair, shoving her in the process.

A silent prayer wrenched through Cat's mind. *Please, help me!* The only thing she could think to do was to keep him talking. She glanced down at her purse. It was only a foot away from her. If she could just get to her phone she might stand a chance. "You left the paper under the rock."

He smirked, a smug look coming over him. "That was a nice touch, don't you think? You were always so caught up in that hero nonsense. I knew that paper would get your attention."

She jerked, the realization hitting her square between the eyes. "You're not Hero."

He belted out a raspy laugh. "No, duh."

Her mind whirled. "H—how?" she blustered. "How did you trick me?" Her mind sifted through the pages of the past, searching for the answer. Suddenly, she knew. "That day when one of the notes blew away in the wind, it went across the schoolyard. You found it."

"Yes, Cat, I did," he said nastily. "Then, I started watching."

Her insides chilled. "You spied on me."

"I saw him put the notes in the tree, if that's what you're asking."

Her breath caught in her throat, curiosity outweighing her fear. "You know who Hero is."

He grunted. "The only 'hero' you need to be worried about is me," he thundered.

The timing of Drew's reappearance was suspicious. Her mind worked to figure out the puzzle. "What connection do you have with Amber?" she demanded. The shocked look on his face let her know she was on the right track. This was crazy! What possible connection could Amber and Drew have?

He smirked. "You've been a naughty girl."

The innuendo in his voice made her skin crawl. Drew was still a handsome man, but he was weak and unprincipled. In other words, he was a scumbag. She shook her head. "What're you talking about?"

"You fell in love with the wrong man and, in the process, made a powerful enemy."

"Amber," she said flatly. Her heart thudded heavily. This whole thing was insane. She'd never even met Amber until today!

"Imagine my surprise when I get a call from a private investigator, asking about you."

A private investigator? Digging into her past? The truth came at her with such force that it nearly stole her breath away. Chase hadn't told Amber anything about Cat's dad. He probably hadn't even known Amber was coming to see her. The whole thing was a setup. Her heart sank as she replayed her accusations on the phone. What must Chase think of her? She realized that Drew was still talking.

"One thing led to another, and before I knew it, Amber hired me for a job."

Her throat closed to the size of a straw. She swallowed to clear it.

"What sort of job?" she squeaked. An icy fear was taking hold of her insides.

"Make her boyfriend believe that you've been running around with me."

"That's absurd," she spat.

A cruel smile twisted over his lips. "We can do this the easy or the hard way."

For a split second, she didn't get it. The synapses of her brain connected when she saw the look in Drew's eyes. Fear—swift and paralyzing—swept through her. Drew planned to rape her. Time turned back, and she felt like she was right back where she started, the night she fled Chicago. She rose from her chair. "Your plan won't work." Her pulse was hammering so erratically that a wave of dizziness assaulted her.

He rose to his feet. "It's interesting how things come together, isn't it Cat?" The sound of his voice was triumphant, like he was getting a thrill out of taunting her. "I'm about to get what you've denied me for years. Now, I'll even get paid for it."

Drew was crazy, twisted. "No one will believe it was consensual."

He laughed. "Oh, I wouldn't be too sure. Amber's a crafty one. With enough money, it's possible to make people believe anything you want them to."

Cat made a run for it. She got only a couple of feet away before Drew caught her ankles, causing her to fall forward. She spun around, scrambling to her feet. He lumbered forward to attack, but she kicked him in the groin. Cursing, he doubled over. Cat went for the door, but before she could get out, Drew caught her in a choke hold. She ground her heel into the top of his foot, causing him to loosen his grasp. She tried to open the door, but he stopped her. She clawed him in the face.

"You'll pay for that," he growled, grabbing her hair.

Hard knocks sounded on the door. "Cat? It's me. Open up."

Tears sprang to Cat's eyes. "Chase!" she screamed. "Inside! Help!"

"'Hero' comes to save the day," Drew sneered. Cat saw the flash of movement, and then felt the blinding streak of pain across her jaw. It went through her mind that Drew had punched her. Stars exploded in her head as she fell …

Cat was swimming in a darkness so complete that she couldn't penetrate it. She saw the tree with the knothole from her childhood. It began to spin, notes flying out of it. Drew's face loomed over her, terrible and taunting. "I'm your hero," he boasted.

"No!" she shouted, tears staining her cheeks. Another image floated in her mind as soft and supple as a palm full of rose petals. She saw his boyish grin, those penetrating blue eyes that could see into the innermost parts of her soul. She was drifting, trying to get through the haze.

"Cat?"

Her heart lifted. She heard his voice. She had to get to him. She had to let him know that she knew the truth.

"Cat, wake up."

Her eyelids fluttered. They were weighted with concrete, impossible to open.

"Cat!"

She opened her eyes, his face coming into focus. "Chase?" Was she dreaming, or was he really here?

He breathed a sigh of relief. "You're okay."

She realized that he was holding her in his arms. For a second, she couldn't get her bearings. Then it all came rushing back. She looked around, the fingers of panic prickling her spine. "Drew?" She and Chase were on the floor, their backs resting against the bottom of the couch.

"We fought. He went down. I called 911. He got up and ran away." Chase pulled her to him. "I'm so glad you're okay," he breathed into the top of her hair.

"Thanks, to you."

He chuckled. "I don't know about that. You looked like you had things under control … slugger."

The admiration in his voice caused her to smile. "I'm surprised you came after I lambasted you."

"That's precisely why I came early, to find out what was going on.

I got Dr. Simpson to cover for me and rushed over as quickly as I could."

"You got here just in the nick of time." Needing to see his face, she pulled back and angled to face him. The movement caused pain to stab through her jaw. "Ouch," she said miserably. "My jaw hurts."

A lopsided grin pulled at his lips. "You should probably have that looked at."

"Yeah, I'll see if I can find a good doctor." Tears glistened in her eyes. "I'm sorry," she croaked, "for all of those things I said over the phone."

His expression was earnest. "I don't know how Amber knew those things about you, but I swear it wasn't from me." His forehead wrinkled in confusion. "Why was Drew O'Hannon here?"

A hysterical laugh rose in her throat. It was too much to contain. Mirth shook her shoulders as it issued out. She laughed in hoarse thrusts, the tension inside her breaking up. She must've looked absolutely ridiculous because Chase frowned. "What?"

She shook her head. "You won't believe it when I tell you."

His eyes held hers, demanding answers. "Try me."

She sucked in a breath. "Amber hired him." His lips parted in surprise. Before he could respond, she rushed on. "She hired Drew to break us up. From what Drew said, Amber was trying to make it look like I was running around with Drew behind your back. Drew took the opportunity to try and rape me." A shudder ran through her. "And, he almost succeeded."

Fury burned in Chase's eyes. "I should've pummeled Drew to a pulp when I had the chance."

Cat figured that Chase had given Drew a good throttling but was too modest to admit it.

Chase's head swung back and forth. "How could Amber be so cold and calculating?"

They heard sirens in the distance. They rose to their feet, looking out the window. A few seconds later, a police car pulled up. Two deputies piled out. After a short round of questions, the deputies took off in search of Drew, promising to come back and take Chase and Cat's statements.

Cat turned to Chase. "So, it would seem that we have some unfinished business ... Hero."

He blinked. "What?"

Tears rose in her eyes. "All this time ... it was you."

He gave her an incredulous look. "How did you know?"

"When you knocked on the door, Drew said that my hero was coming to save me. Suddenly, everything clicked, and I knew."

He flashed a sheepish grin. "I guess the secret's out. I've always had a thing for you, Cat."

She touched his jaw. "Why didn't you say anything?"

"I was too chicken. You were larger than life ... so take charge ... ready to face down any bully. Even Drew O'Hannon. I wanted to muster the courage to tell you ... was working my way around to it, but then you put the rock in the knothole."

"I never did that." Anger rose in her breast, thinking of all the things Drew had taken from her.

His head snapped up. "Huh?"

Regret filled her. "That was Drew O'Hannon."

He shook his head. "I don't understand."

She let out a long, heavy sigh. "Drew found one of your notes. He pretended to be Hero."

His eyes widened before his brows darted down in a sharp V. "Is that why you started dating him?"

She nodded.

Chase's features tightened in an agonized expression. She could feel the pain and anger simmering inside him. "I'm so sorry." He grunted. "I'm such an idiot!" He searched her face. "Can you ever forgive me?"

"There's nothing to forgive." She thought of something Amber said, her stomach tightening. "Chase, Amber said that you gave up a position at St. Mark's Hospital for me. Is that true?"

"No," he responded instantly, making a face. "I never wanted that position. I told Amber that in no uncertain terms." He paused. "She was determined to dictate my life." His lips formed grim lines. "I knew Amber was spoiled and pampered, but I had no idea that she would stoop to such levels to get her way."

"It almost worked." Tears misted her eyes. She was so grateful that she'd been protected from greater harm. Simply being here with Chase, learning that he was literally the hero of her dreams filled Cat with elation. Earlier, she'd been in the depths of despair, and now she was flying high. "What a day," she said with a shaky laugh.

He gathered her hands into his. "Let's make a pact. From here on out, nothing ever separates us again."

His beautiful eyes brimmed with such intensity and tenderness that it shot a glow of joy straight through her heart. "Agreed," she said firmly. Notwithstanding her sore jaw, she needed a kiss. "My real hero," she murmured as her lips sought his.

EPILOGUE

Two years later ...

Cat's stomach churned like it held a bucket of butterflies as she clenched and unclenched her hands. "Take a deep breath," Chase urged, placing a hand over hers. "Your hands are ice."

"I know. Sorry."

He pulled his eyes off the road long enough to give her a reassuring look. "You've got this."

She nodded, sucking in a deep breath. "I don't know why I'm getting so worked up about this," she lamented.

"It's a big deal. You haven't been home in eight years."

In some ways, it felt like it had been longer than eight years. Other times, it felt like it was only yesterday. Cat often dreamt of the house she'd grown up in and Mami. Sometimes, she'd catch a whiff of a sweet musky scent that reminded her of Mami and the memories would flood her. During those times, she could almost feel Mami standing beside her, wrapping her thin arms around Cat and placing a motherly kiss on her forehead. Tears misted her eyes as she blinked, forcing her mind onto another topic. This was a happy day. She was excited about going home and didn't want to end up breaking into tears before they even got to the neighborhood.

She angled toward Chase. "It must feel pretty good to come back home as Dr. Chase Brooks." She grinned thinking of how distinguished Chase had looked standing tall and proud in his green and black convocation gown with the red, white, and blue hood. The graduation had taken place a week prior, and his parents had flown in for the occasion. Over the past couple of years, since she and Chase had been together, Cat had gotten to know Chase's parents. They were warm and accepting, welcoming Cat with open arms into their family. Cat was grateful for the association. It was nice to be part of a family again. She looked forward to the time when Chase's parents would officially become her in-laws, even though she'd secretly thought them as such for some time now. Cat and Chase talked constantly about the future, but they'd decided to wait until after Chase graduated to get engaged. Cat hoped Chase wouldn't wait too long to propose because she longed to be Mrs. Chase Brooks with all her heart.

For a time, Cat fretted over where Chase's career might take him. She loved her dance studio, Harper and her crew, and the community of Clementine. Cat didn't want to leave. However, she was prepared to do so if necessary. Then, Chase told her the wonderful news that he was doing his internship and residency at the hospital in Daphne. When she'd questioned if that's what he wanted to do, he'd replied with a glib, "How would South Alabama dance if we moved away?" She could see the tenderness beneath the teasing and knew that he was choosing Daphne because of her. Knowing that Chase was considerate of Cat's needs and wants meant the world to her. Her gaze moved over his handsome features. Sometimes, she had to pinch herself to make sure she was awake. She never knew that life and love could be so wonderful.

They were almost there. She looked out the window, taking in the familiar buildings and landscape. She was surprised at how crowded everything was compared to the open space of Clementine.

"It feels strange, doesn't it?" Chase remarked.

"Yes, and so familiar." Cat felt like she'd changed so much and yet everything looked the same. Her thoughts went to Drew O'Hannon as tight strings pulled across her stomach. Drew was arrested the night he tried to rape her and was serving a three year prison sentence. Cat had to go to court and testify against him. It was grueling emotionally, but she'd made it through it with Chase by her side. Facing Drew in court, realizing that he had to accept the consequences of his actions, helped her put closure on the situation. Cat was glad that Drew was still in prison. That way, she had no fear of running into him during this trip. Amber was questioned in the incident but never prosecuted. She claimed to have no knowledge of Drew's intent to rape Cat. Cat didn't know if she believed that, but that was neither here nor there. Cat was just glad the sordid mess was over.

When they turned onto Cat's street, her pulse skyrocketed. She held her breath as they pulled in front of her old home. The brick house looked nearly the same except for the moss green awnings over the front door and bay window. The awnings were faded with age, making Cat realize how much time had actually passed. She surveyed the yard, her eyes settling on the leafy tree with the knothole. Emotion lodged in her throat as her eyes met Chase's. She could tell from his expression that he was reading her thoughts.

"We've come full circle," he said, giving her a tender smile.

"Yes, we have," she agreed.

Chase reached for her hand and squeezed it. "You ready?"

"Yes," she smiled.

He came around and opened her door. Cat got out, smoothing her hand down her blouse. She'd not told her former neighbor Romina Castaneda that she was coming. Chase placed his hand in the small of Cat's back, leading her up the walkway. Did Romina still live here? Was she still alive? She pushed the doorbell and waited. A few seconds later, they heard movement.

The door opened and Romina was there. When she saw Cat, her face brightened with recognition, tears rushing to her eyes. "Carmelita," she exclaimed, her arms outstretched. "You've finally come home."

"Yes," Cat uttered, choking back her emotion as the two embraced in a tight hug. Surprisingly, Romina didn't look much different than Cat remembered, perhaps a few more lines on her face, but that was all.

Romina ushered them in to have a cup of tea. It was wonderful catching up on news about Cat's former neighbors. "I have something for you," Cat said.

"What?" Romina asked, looking surprised.

Cat reached into her purse and pulled out an envelope filled with money. She rose from her seat and placed it into Romina's aged hands. "You can't know what it meant to me to have this money. Thank you. It gave me a fresh start ... a new life."

Tears pooled in Romina's eyes, fogging up her glasses. "I was glad to do it. It was a gift, not a loan." There was a hint of reproof in her tone.

"I know, but I'm doing well now, and I wanted to repay your kindness. If you don't need it, give it to someone who does."

Romina's thin lips pressed into a smile. "Your mother would be proud of the fine person you've become."

"Thank you," Cat said, fighting tears.

Chase's phone rang. He pulled it out. "It's my mother, probably wondering if we're in town yet." He got up. "Excuse me." He went to the front door and stepped outside to take the call.

Cat sat back down.

"You got a good one," Romina said with an impish grin that peeled back the ravages of time, making her look like a young girl.

"Yes."

Romina winked. "He's a dapper one."

A giggle rumbled in Cat's throat. "Yes, he is."

A few minutes later, Chase stepped back in with an apologetic grin. "Sorry about that. Mom's excited about having us." Cat and Chase were spending a few days with Chase's parents.

After chatting another half hour, Cat scooted to the edge of her seat. "Well, we'd better get going." They said goodbye to Romina, promising to keep in better touch this time. As they went to the car, Cat cast a final glance at her old home. A feeling of nostalgia wafted over her. She didn't feel as much sadness as she'd expected. Mostly, just gratitude for her wonderful, scrappy mother who'd carved out a life for them despite overwhelming obstacles. *I love you, Mami.*

Chase placed his hand on the passenger door to open it for Cat. Then, he paused cocking his head.

"What?"

A sparkle rippled through his blue eyes. "You know we can't leave here without checking the knothole."

She laughed in surprise. "Are you serious?"

His face split into a large smile, revealing his dimple. "Why not. It's tradition."

She shook her head, grinning. "Alright, Hero, let's do it. One last time." They walked hand-in-hand to the tree. "Do you want to do the honors, or should I?"

"I'll go first," he said quickly as he reached in. His eyes widened. "There's something here."

She leaned forward. "What?" He pulled out his hand. Laughter gurgled in her throat when she saw the Matchbox car in the palm of his hand. "Well, it seems that you and I aren't the only ones who left treasures in the knothole."

"Alright, slugger. Your turn." He winked. "For tradition."

"Okay." Dutifully she reached inside, not expecting to find anything. Her brows crinkled. "Wait, there's something else." Her hand clasped around a box and pulled it out. It was a small, black, square box. She looked at Chase who was watching her expectantly. Hope rose in her breast. "Is this?"

"Open it," he encouraged.

She did so, a soft gasp escaping her lips. Tears welled in her eyes as she reached for the diamond ring and slipped it onto her finger. It was a perfect fit. Chase knew her so well. He got down on one knee, peering up at her. "Carmelita Andrea Anastasia Hernandez de Silva. I've loved you all my life. Will you marry me?"

Some instinctual part of her had picked Chase out from the very beginning, all those years ago. "Yes," she exclaimed, laughing as tears rolled down her cheeks. She looked toward Romina's house and realized she was standing on the porch, watching.

Chase rose to his feet. Cat threw down the empty ring box and flung her arms around his neck. "I love you, Hero," she exclaimed with throaty emotion.

"I love you too. And for the record, you're my hero. It has always been you."

As their lips met in a kiss, Cat caught the faint scent of sweet musk in the air and felt more than heard a whisper of Mami's gentle laughter. Somehow in a way she couldn't explain, she knew that Mami was here with them, rejoicing. Romina was right, Cat had finally returned home.

YOUR FREE BOOK AWAITS ...

Hey there, thanks for taking the time to read *Dancing With the Doc*. If you enjoyed it, please take a minute to give me a review on Amazon. I really appreciate your feedback, as I depend largely on word of mouth to promote my books.

To receive updates when more of my books are coming out, sign up for my newsletter:

http://bit.ly/freebookjenniferyoungblood

If you sign up for my newsletter, I'll give you one of my books, Beastly Charm: A contemporary retelling of beauty & the beast, for FREE. Plus, you'll get information on discounts and other freebies. Sign up at:

http://bit.ly/freebookjenniferyoungblood

BOOKS BY JENNIFER YOUNGBLOOD

Billionaire Boss Romance
   Her Blue Collar Boss
   Her Lost Chance Boss

Georgia Patriots Romance
   The Hot Headed Patriot
   The Twelfth Hour Patriot
   The Unstoppable Patriot

O'Brien Family Romance
   The Impossible Groom (Chas O'Brien)
   The Twelfth Hour Patriot (McKenna O'Brien)
   The Stormy Warrior (Caden O'Brien and Tess Eisenhart)

Christmas
   Rewriting Christmas (A Novella)
   Yours By Christmas (Park City Firefighter Romance)
   Her Crazy Rich Fake Fiancé

Navy SEAL Romance

The Resolved Warrior
The Reckless Warrior
The Diehard Warrior
The Stormy Warrior

The Jane Austen Pact
Seeking Mr. Perfect

Texas Titan Romances
The Hometown Groom
The Persistent Groom
The Ghost Groom
The Jilted Billionaire Groom
The Impossible Groom
The Perfect Catch (Last Play Series)

Hawaii Billionaire Series
Love Him or Lose Him
Love on the Rocks
Love on the Rebound
Love at the Ocean Breeze
Love Changes Everything
Loving the Movie Star
Love Under Fire (A Companion book to the Hawaii Billionaire Series)

Kisses and Commitment Series
How to See With Your Heart

Angel Matchmaker Series
Kisses Over Candlelight
The Cowboy and the Billionaire's Daughter

Romantic Thrillers
False Identity

False Trust
Promise Me Love
Burned

Contemporary Romance
Beastly Charm

Fairytale Retellings (The Grimm Laws Series)
Banish My Heart **(This book is FREE)**
The Magic in Me
Under Your Spell
A Love So True

Southern Romance
Livin' in High Cotton
Recipe for Love
The Secret Song of the Ditch Lilies

Short Stories
The Southern Fried Fix

Falling for the Doc Series (Co-written with Craig Depew, MD.)
Cooking with the Doc
Dancing with the Doc

The St. Claire Sisters Romance Series (Co-written with Haley Hopkins)
Meet Me in London

ABOUT THE AUTHORS

Jennifer loves reading and writing clean romance. She believes that happily ever after is not just for stories. Jennifer enjoys interior design, rollerblading, clogging, jogging, and chocolate. In Jennifer's opinion there are few ills that can't be solved with a warm brownie and scoop of vanilla-bean ice cream.

Jennifer grew up in rural Alabama and loved living in a town where "everybody knows everybody." Her love for writing began as a young teenager when she wrote stories for her high school English teacher to critique.

Jennifer has BA in English and Social Sciences from Brigham Young University where she served as Miss BYU Hawaii in 1989. Before becoming an author, she worked as the owner and editor of a monthly newspaper named *The Senior Times*.

She now lives in the Rocky Mountains with her family and spends her time writing and doing all of the wonderful things that make up the life of a busy wife and mother.

≈

Craig Depew was born in Edmonton, Alberta. His family moved frequently while he was growing each time his dad earned a job promotion. He lived in much of the eastern half of the United States and Canada and after high school lived in Israel, Japan and Grenada. He went to college at BYU and graduated from medical school at Texas Tech. He spent the first half of his medical career outside Atlanta, GA, and then three more years in Statesboro before moving his practice to the Rocky Mountains of Utah, where he continues seeing patients.

In his writing he draws on the places he's lived and visited, people he's known, and news stories that readers will recognize in his work. He began working on his first novel, Missing, Presumed Dead, in 2000 and finished it about three years later. His second novel, Weightless, won Best in Show at the 2013 League of Utah Writers Creative Writing Competition and his third, Transparent, won Honorable Mention in the same contest.

Made in the USA
Coppell, TX
04 December 2019

12348274R00085